Summer on
Wild Horse Island

Summer on Wild Horse Island

Mary Elwyn Patchett

illustrated by
Roger Payne

Meredith Press, New York

First U.S. edition

Library of Congress Catalog Card Number: 67-14751
Manufactured in the United States of America for Meredith Press

Contents

*Summer on
Wild Horse Island*

1
The Voyage

Oh, look! Sharks!" Danny Delaney's brown eyes shone in her pale face as she pointed to two black triangles that cut through the glass-smooth waters of the Great Barrier Reef, beyond where the wash of the *Captain Cook* fanned back from her prow.

"There are some more!" David, Danny's brother, pointed at two more triangles. Captain Morris, coming along the deck with his first mate, Mr. Reece, smiled when David shouted, "Gee whiz! The sea's full of sharks!"

Across the clear, pale water the tiny sails cruised about, making a miniature regatta, each wide-apart pair moving in unison. Below the triangles were the shadows of shapeless bodies.

"They must be drilling!" said Captain Morris.

"You're lucky," Mr. Reece put in. "Those sails don't belong to sharks but to young rays, I think—look!"

A dark shadow rose, lifting itself, and the triangles broke the surface. A white underside flashed and water streamed like diamonds off the back of a big ray. The curved body was like a black carpet being shaken after washing, and the triangles were the tips of the fleshy "wings." As one ray flopped back another rose, shone darkly for a moment, and hit the surface with a loud slap. Then the water closed over it again. At the children's feet Pauli, the little dachshund, began to bark.

"What're they doing?" David asked, while Danny watched, fascinated.

"They're playing. Look, they'll jump again."

"These aren't so big—some rays are more than twenty feet across their wings. Later you'll see the reefs, like coral walls, close together, but here the outer reef is a long way off, and it makes a playground for the big fish."

"Dad calls the Reef one of the wonders of the world. He says it goes on for twelve hundred and fifty miles."

Captain Morris nodded. "Yes, and Captain Cook was the first man to navigate it. Even he hit a reef."

Across the silken sea the setting sun made the water glow like rose-colored glass. Far out they saw the purple line of the outer reef. Between it and the ship the water held streaks of color—deep blues, greens, and wine-dark stains, like crushed grapes. In the heat the children's faces looked as though a shower had drenched them; their shirts stuck to their bodies. The rays disappeared, and the Captain and the Mate stopped beside the chairs where the elder Delaneys snoozed.

"Feeling stronger, Mrs. Delaney?" the Captain asked. Mr. Delaney dozed on, but Mrs. Delaney smiled.

"Every day makes a difference," she said. "The doctor

said it'll be six months before we're ourselves again. The children got off more lightly, thank goodness."

Out of earshot the Captain said grimly, "When I look at that family I'm glad I drive a ship and not a car. They were taking a bend when a fool driver came by on the wrong side and forced Delaney's car over the edge. The driver went on. Delaney and his missus were badly smashed up, the children less badly."

"It's a miracle they weren't all killed."

"They've got guts, those kids. Danny came to first, her mother told me, and she turned off the engine or they'd all have been burned alive."

"Not bad for an eleven-year-old."

"David did all right for a thirteen-year-old. He was badly cut, but he walked, or crawled, on a sprained ankle, and got help. That saved his parents."

"Six months camped on a beach and they won't know themselves." Mr. Reece climbed the ladder to the bridge.

Pauli wriggled her sleek body, imploring the children to tell her what was going on in the big bath out there. Danny picked her up, and the dog lay back like a lazy baby, tummy upmost, floppy paws dangling.

"Daniela," Mrs. Delaney protested, "I'm sure Pauli's too heavy; put her here."

Pauli licked Danny's chin and closed her eyes blissfully. "She's not heavy, Mother," Danny said. "We're taking her to visit the horses down below."

Mr. Delaney opened a sleepy eye. "Hello, kids."

"We saw big rays playing!" David told him.

"Why didn't you wake me?"

"Mother says we're not to wake you for six months!"

His father smiled. "I sound like a sort of junior Rip van Winkle, the way you put it," he said.

"Dad, why are the horses in the hold called 'walers'?"

"Because that's what the Indian Army men called the big, bony, weight-carrying horses from New South Wales."

David nodded. "There are only eight horses down below now," he said, "but they used to carry up to sixty in the old days."

"It's a wonder they can take eight with all our junk! Outboard, dinghy, tents, books, and everything!"

Danny chuckled. "I'm glad now that we couldn't fly," she said.

Mr. Delaney watched his children's backs disappearing down the companionway. "Oh, for half their energy! I just want to sleep."

"We both do," replied his wife, "and it *is* hot; I hope camping won't be too strenuous."

"Of course not! Not with all our labor-saving gear."

At night the sea was full of enchantment. The water streamed back in glassy darkness, its surface lit by the deck lights. Changing surface patterns showed when a great body moved close to the ship. Deep down, sheets of blue flame glowed, alight with cold fire, and the children knew that these were giant jellyfish.

Early one morning, standing on the bridge, Danny called, "Come and look—the tiniest island!" She pointed to where a brownish-green hump rose above the water.

"That's not an island, my dear, it's the back of a green turtle enjoying the early sunshine."

"Won't we ride those on the reef?"

"If you're lucky. The old sailing ships carried them for food, because turtles can live for months without eating. The hawksbill isn't quite as big as the green. It's hunted

for tortoiseshell. The leathery turtle they call the luth is the biggest—he's soft-shelled. Not many left now."

"It's exciting seeing new animals!" Danny's face fell, for the accident had left her easily depressed. "Oh, dear, we'll soon be leaving the ship, and I do love it."

Green islets and coral cays were left behind. The

coastline turned into rugged cliffs, with here and there the thin white threads of sandy beaches. The mighty shoulder of Cape Tribulation, named by Captain Cook, rose from the sea sixty miles north of Cairns. The sea turned to a choppy dark green, and gray ghosts of rain swept like gauzy veils across it. Cooktown lay only an hour or so northward.

"You look terrible," said David, peering down at Danny.

Danny glanced at her rather grimy shirt and shorts, and said crossly, "I don't care. I don't want to go ashore much." She felt her eyes sting. She never used to be so silly. She bent down so that David wouldn't see and tickled Pauli's golden velvet tummy. Then she went along the deck and Pauli followed. Danny's friend Larry was polishing brasswork. He wiped his forehead, leaving a greasy black stain on it, and waved his cleaning rag at the shore.

"That's Mount Cook," he said. "That one with the green peak. You'll soon see Archer Point Lighthouse, at the river entrance."

The *Captain Cook* rolled and plunged, wallowing through the Pacific swell driven across the outer reef. Danny staggered a little, bracing herself against the movement. Pauli's short, broad-pawed legs rode the deck as if she were an old salt. She leaped onto Mr. Delaney's knees and knocked his book on the deck. Danny picked it up.

"You're very naughty, you mustn't wake Dad," said Danny severely.

"She didn't wake me." Mr. Delaney rubbed Pauli's ears.

Danny thought, "How white and thin he looks."

Mr. Delaney went on, "I was reading about Cooktown in the gold-rush days of 1873. It was a sea of canvas for thirty thousand people, and now there are only a few hundred people living there."

"What did all those people eat?" Danny perched herself gingerly on the footrest.

"What Captain Cook ate, kangaroo. He was the first white man to taste it. But the kangaroos were soon killed off. The tens of thousands of Chinese there wanted rice. When the famine really began, the whites wouldn't let them in, so ships put them ashore down the coast. Lines of Chinese with pigtails and bags of rice fought their way over the mountains and through the rain forest. Thousands died or were speared by Aboriginals. Gold has always been bought with men's lives. In the end the miners ate their dogs and horses; then they boiled their boots and ate those too; yet many of those starving men had tins filled with gold."

"How awful. I couldn't eat Pauli! May we go ashore?"

"Yes, if there's time."

"All right then, I'd better get dressed up."

The Delaneys laughed as Danny disappeared below. "Dressed up indeed! That means a clean shirt at most!"

The ship moved slowly beside the wharf. Cooktown lay in a vast bowl of encircling hills, with the mangrove-fringed banks of the Endeavour River at one side. Shipping dotted the river. Two squat, black pearling luggers from Thursday Island swung on the mirror of the water. A freighter from Hong Kong and several sugar boats rocked on the swell, with their dinghys, or rowboats, attached, like monstrous browsing beasts followed by their young.

On the wharf a small crowd gathered, the white men in limp tropical clothing; Aboriginals grinned at the children, who smiled back. The black women wore sleazy cotton dresses and many of the children were naked.

Danny said eagerly, "Oh, come on, David!"

The children ran down the gangway and along the wharf. Pauli galloped after them, her paws throwing dust up onto her low-clearance chest. She bounced gaily around, her ears flapping and her ratlike tail making whirling circles.

The children found Charlotte Street lined with dark-leaved mango trees. Its junk shops, filled with colorful oriental trash, were squeezed between old houses and vacant lots. When they reached the Captain Cook monument David said, "We'd better go back. Dad'll worry."

Danny nodded, calling, "Pauli! Pauli!"

"Hurry, Danny, we'll be late."

They arrived, panting, at the wharf and clattered over rough boards and between boxes of freight, steel kegs of beer, tins of kerosene, and all the off-loaded cargo of the *Captain Cook*. The three scrambled up the gangway to join the elder Delaneys.

Holding Pauli in her arms, Danny leaned over the rails.

"My word, you only just made it," Mr. Delaney told his children.

The engines throbbed and the deck vibrated gently. Sailors moved about, slipping the moorings, until the big gangway was drawn away.

The sky was dark and the ship rolled and staggered through heavy seas. In the saloon after dinner David peered from a porthole at the starless sky. Through the blackness of the night it seemed as if the air made a heavy, deep silence about them. Through it they heard the rattle of the anchor chain.

"I suppose we're in the lee of a headland," Mr. Delaney remarked.

It wasn't long before the storm broke. First it announced itself with the moaning of a far-off wind. Then it crashed about them, shrieking and banging the ship as if all the fiends of the air had set upon it. It was a tiring night with the continuous movement and the harsh, screaming noises. Danny and David worried about the cargo of horses carried below, and they spent most of the night helping to quiet them. David, as he had done so often before, marveled again at the power to quiet down animals which his sister possessed. He was thoroughly competent with horses and other animals, but Danny was something more. Others noticed it, but no one, and certainly not Danny, knew what it was that existed between her and a frightened beast. That night she moved quietly from horse to horse as the hold creaked and tilted and groaned. Wherever Danny was, that horse settled down beneath her touch.

Toward morning the worst of the storm passed, and David and Danny, unable to sleep, went up on deck. The darkness thinned and a figure appeared from far up the deck. They could just make out Captain Morris walking toward them.

"Hello, kids, you're up early," he called.

"We thought we might never see another cyclone."

"I'm on my way to my cabin for coffee. Like to come?"

"Oh, yes, we'd love to, thanks."

The hot coffee was pleasant after the long night. Both

children felt sleepy, but refused to go to their cabins until it was full daylight and they could look around and see the results of the cyclone.

Just as they were finishing their coffee they heard a sharp rap on the door. The Captain rose and opened it. A sailor stood outside and said something to the Captain that the children could not hear. Then the sailor grinned at them through the door and went off.

"Sometimes cyclones bring funny things into ships," said Captain Morris, turning toward them. "Johnson says our ship's no exception. If you want to see what he found, you'd better come along with me. I've an idea you'll be interested."

2

Percy Joins the Family

The cyclone-strewn debris and the decks of the *Captain Cook* glistened with water. Deckhands had begun swabbing at the far end of the deck. Danny and David followed the Captain carefully, wondering what the surprise was that he had promised them.

The children's feet were bare, and they avoided stepping on mysterious pieces of seaweed. Any piece could hide some stinging creature, hurled aboard from the teeming waters of the Great Barrier Reef by the fierce wind of the cyclone the night before. Danny stopped and bent down to look under a piece of moving seaweed to find a couple of small crabs hiding in its dank strands. Small fish flapped on the water-soaked deck and Danny threw a couple overboard.

"You'd better not do that," Captain Morris said. "You might wish you had some fish in a minute!"

The two children ran to catch up with him. David was the first to see what looked like an untidy bundle of black-edged white laundry, pushed into a sheltered angle of the deck.

"What's that?" David asked.

The Captain smiled. "That's what I've brought you to see!" he said. "Quietly now, it could have a broken leg or wing."

David stood back, but Danny went toward the big bedraggled bird. Something made the Captain stand back too.

"Be careful, Danny," the Captain warned her. "It might peck you—"

"Danny'll be all right," David said proudly. "She can do anything with animals."

He and the Captain watched Danny move quietly beside the big bundle of feathers. She put out her hand and touched it gently. The ragged bundle heaved convulsively and Danny bent forward and spoke soothingly. Presently the shape of a large untidy bird emerged from the muddle of black and white feathers.

"Why—it's a pelican!" David said excitedly.

"Yes, the cyclone blew it aboard last night. Johnson found it. We've had them before and they're generally more exhausted than hurt. One of them did have a broken wing and we kept it aboard. It traveled with us for about a year before it disappeared one day."

Danny knelt beside the pelican and smoothed its big

pinions. It was David who jumped as it suddenly turned its head and the great beak made a clacking sound over Danny's shoulder. She looked into a round eye at the side of its head, and it stared back, unafraid. Very carefully, with the Captain and her brother watching, Danny felt the big wings and decided they were sound. Then her hands burrowed through the under feathers to find the legs of the crouching bird. The big pelican moved coyly and wagged its head as if she were tickling it. Finally Danny decided the legs, too, were unbroken and that it must be just exhausted and perhaps bruised by the cyclone. She sat back.

"I think he's only sore and hungry," she said. "Pelicans are always hungry, so let's get the old boy some breakfast."

"I told you not to throw the fish overboard!"

Captain Morris went back to the bridge while the children borrowed a basket from the galley and almost filled it with stranded fish and crabs. Carrying the well-filled bucket between them, they staggered back with it. They laughed at the greedy look in the round eyes peering at them as a fish slithered to the deck and was put back again.

"I believe he knows these are for him."

"Of course he does, just look!"

The untidy bundle sorted itself out, and it was unmistakably a very big bird, and pleased with its new home. Because pelicans are almost dumb, it merely shook its head and rattled its beak, grabbing fish after fish from the children.

"Hey, Danny! Save some. Goodness knows when we'll get more food for it!"

"Oh, but he must be hungry. We'll think of some way to get more."

As fast as one fish disappeared the big beak opened

for another. "He must be absolutely stuffed," Danny said in awed tones as they came to the last fish, which the pelican took but did not swallow. It held the fish's head in its beak so that the tail flopped outside. Then it raised itself a little and shook its big body until it made room, and the fish disappeared.

"There, now you have a sleep, and we'll ask the sailors not to disturb you, and later we'll try and get you some lunch."

The round golden eyes looked at them owlishly; then they closed, and the big bird settled its neck in a graceful S-bend and proceeded to doze off. Danny rose to her feet.

"I think I'll go and find Pauli."

"Better try Mother's cabin. I'll come too."

Pauli felt splendid after a long night's rest in possession of most of Mrs. Delaney's bunk. Danny was much firmer with her than her mother was. She insisted that Pauli must stay on her own side of the bunk, and Pauli found it was no use settling herself with her four short legs against Danny's back and pushing hard. But Mrs. Delaney's resistance to Pauli's charms was weak. She felt flattered when Pauli stayed with her and always found herself pushed to the very edge. Now the little dog was drowsy and sweet with sleep. She rolled on her back and flopped her paws helplessly at Danny. Mrs. Delaney tickled one fat paw.

"Did you both have a good sleep?" she asked Danny.

David grinned wickedly and sat beside Danny on the edge of the bunk. "We stayed with the horses most of the night."

"Oh, you dreadful children! You must have a long sleep sometime today."

"Oh, Mother, we can sleep when we get ashore. Captain Morris says he'll be landing us tomorrow morning."

"Then you must rest and be ready to make camp."

The day passed like a dream. An aftermath of the cyclone, the great movement of the Pacific Ocean washing across the reefs, seemed to swell the shining waters. It was as if some giant glassblower crouched beneath the ocean and blew the water almost to the bursting point, then let it subside when he drew another breath. The water had a compressed look, and the storm had stirred up clouds of sand and debris, muddying water that was normally crystal clear.

Cliffs rose from the rugged shore. Later this harshness lessened. The white threads of beaches widened, the hills flattened, and the tropical bush brought its tangle of green right to the edge of the sand.

One of the sailors produced a net so that Percy Pelican—as they had decided to call him—could be fed. The children started with the idea that a netful of fish three times a day ought to satisfy any pelican. They soon discovered their mistake. Percy's reproachful eyes met them wherever they went along the deck, saying plainly, "I'm *starving!*" So on the last day they did very little except pack Percy inwardly. That night both children slept soundly.

Although it had been their last night aboard, Mrs. Delaney did not have to insist on their going to bed early. Their eyes drooped and they smothered huge yawns even before supper was over. Then they fell into their bunks and slept soundly.

Danny woke first. The problem of Percy's breakfast sprang at once to her mind. She jumped from her bunk and rushed off to shower and dress, ready to get one of their sailor friends to help cope with the fishing. She did not dare walk along Percy's side of the deck and meet those reproachful eyes when the cupboard was bare!

With the aid of a net, trawled along the side of the ship, she filled a bucket. A shining, glistening fish fell from the bucket, and Danny put it overboard. Percy disapproved. She picked up another fish, put it in the bucket, and went toward him.

The pelican sat humped like a miniature snowy mountain, except that his snow was contained by the black on his back and along the edges of his wings. He waddled a few steps out of his shelter, enjoying the pale early morning sunshine. When Danny drew near he turned his head and clacked his beak at her reproachfully.

Down went the fish at incredible speed, while an occasional one was left in the big pouch, evidently to be savored later during the starvation period while Danny trawled for his lunch! Mr. Delaney walked along the deck. Percy had rearranged his storm-blown feathers into their usual tidy pattern, flat and sleek to his body, in the way that falconers call "hard penned." Conscious that he was being admired, Percy spread his sturdy legs and raised his wings. Danny felt alarmed that he might be going to fly away, but he only stood and flapped.

"Pelicans are the finest soarers in the world," her father told her. "Their wings are eleven times as long as they are broad, which means they have to flap them very little to keep floating on the air currents, once they are high enough."

"How long would Percy's be, Daddy?"

"Oh, I should think about five feet. He's certainly a very big bird."

"He ought to be; look how he eats!"

Mr. Delaney laughed and asked, "Are you two sorry to be leaving the ship?"

"Oh, yes, we are. But it looks lovely and lonely around here and we're longing to see our own beach."

"Come along, then, you'd better get your packing done. Don't leave it all for your mother."

As they turned from the rail Percy threw them the reproachful look of a pelican who doesn't know where his next meal is coming from. He waddled a few steps after them before giving up and settling down to contemplate the harshness of his life.

Before noon the children felt the throb of the engines lessening. They knew they must be opposite the beach that was to be their home for the next six months. They leaned over the rail and looked at the broad sweep of pale sand before them, half a mile of it between the headlands of tumbled rocks and the background of massed tropical greens. They were pleased to see several coconut palms. Coconuts do not grow naturally in Australia, but the palms have sprung up when the nuts have washed ashore from cargoes, or have been planted by natives from outer islands.

Danny thought that Percy would fly off at any moment, but Percy knew when he had a good thing. As she and David stood together she could hear the clacking of his beak above the rattle of the anchor chain and other shipboard noises. She went along the deck to the companionway that led to the bridge, ran up it, and asked if she could stay.

The Captain smiled. "What do you want to do about Percy?" he asked. "He'll have to do his own fishing if he comes with us."

"Can't we take him ashore with us?"

"Yes, if he doesn't fly off."

"I think there must be pools in those rocks at the end of the beach. Could he feed himself from those?"

"No doubt he *could,* but I doubt if he *will*. Percy knows a sucker when he sees one!"

"Anyway, we can't leave him behind—he's one of the family. Even Pauli's friendly with him."

The Delaneys watched their camping equipment being

loaded into ship's boats. Their dinghy and the outboard were fastened behind it. Mr. Delaney went with the first load to choose the site for the tents, and the family went next.

When the time came for them to leave the ship, the boat was swinging lazily on the tide below them, and Danny and David felt a peculiar sinking of their spirits. They had loved life on the *Captain Cook,* their friends who manned the ship, and the horses they had helped to look after. Now all that was ending and a new life lay before them.

They forgot their doubts and regrets when Percy, bulging with fish, refused to be any help at all to what he thought of as foolish people who wouldn't let a man digest his dinner in peace. No amount of cajolery from Danny moved him. The men became so fed up with Percy's uncooperative attitude that in the end they lifted him bodily, his knobbly legs sticking out like yellow pegs, and his beak clacking. With his feathers fluffed he looked huge as they dumped him in the boat. He sank to the bottom like a lead-weighted toy, but Percy's weights were not made of lead, they were his luncheon fish.

When they reached the beach, the process of moving Percy began all over again. Finally Danny found him a nice spot with the wall of her tent at his back, and Percy settled in like some clucky old hen. She gave him a few fish just to soothe his ruffled feelings. By midafternoon the camp was set up and in apple-pie order. Then came farewells to all the helpers, and the Captain came over to tea.

At five o'clock Captain Morris said good-bye and returned to his ship to catch the tide. The children watched her moving out into the channel with mixed feelings. She turned north, and they ran along the half-mile of beach and stood on the far headland, waving to their friends.

When the ship was just a black dot in the distance they turned to each other, and David said, "Let's watch for another minute; then we'll go along the next beach. See, it's only a short one. We can look from those rocks."

The ship was too far out to be seen properly by then, but that last look, they decided later, was the most fateful of their lives. It was standing on that rocky headland, with the sea of melted emerald all about them, that they first saw the island that later came to be called "Wild Horse."

3

The Terror of Wild Horse Island

Danny and David each had a small sleeping tent and a cot with a mosquito net hanging over it. Danny woke at sunrise with Pauli snuggled into her back, but she had the unusual feeling that there was someone else in her tent. She was quite right. The weight that had pulled the mosquito net to one side was Percy's. Obviously he had felt lonely and had waddled into her tent when she was too sound asleep to notice. Now, when she moved, he began clattering his beak as a sort of breakfast bell, reminding her that he was feeling a bit peckish.

Pauli woke and yapped excitedly. When she peered through the net and saw that it was only Percy, she retired to sleep again in the curve of Danny's arm.

"Oh, dear!" Danny thought. "This is awful. Feeding Percy will take up all my time—I won't even be able to go along and explore that lovely island we saw, because Percy will be wanting more and more fish."

She heard David calling, "Come on, Danny, let's have a swim."

She pushed Pauli aside and ran to the tent flap and peered out. David stood in the pale splendor of the morning, warm air and early sunshine breaking over him. Behind him was the lovely curve of the beach, and the sea was a sparkling, rippling sheet of blue and emerald. David was wearing his swimming trunks.

"I don't see how I can have a swim," Danny said. "Percy wants his breakfast. Listen to him!"

"Never mind Percy! Let him get it, or I'll help you later. Come on, now—just look at that sea."

Percy clattered disapprovingly and Pauli raced excitedly across the beach. Danny followed David into the placid sea. It had turned to a pale jade and was crystal clear now that the cyclone debris had settled. Both children swam exceptionally well, but as David was thirteen and Danny only eleven, he was stronger in the water, although she was almost as fast when it came to racing. They splashed and shouted, ducking each other, churning the water into two frothy lines as they swam a fast racing crawl.

Then, some way from shore, but bringing a menace that both children respected, they saw a small black triangle cutting the surface. A shark moved in the waters. Perhaps it was a small one, but it could still be deadly. They came out and threw themselves on the sand to dry off. Mr. Delaney came over to them, carrying his towel.

"Hello, Dad! It's marvelous in there. We came out because we saw a shark fin. It was a long way out and it's gone now, though."

Mr. Delaney nodded. "Good boy," he said. "Don't

take chances. It's so calm there are no breaking waves to keep them out. Your mother and I will have a quick dip near the shore."

The children let their bathing suits dry on them as they ran about collecting wood for the breakfast fire. As fast as they made a heap of dry sticks Pauli scattered them, but she was having such fun no one could bear to scold her. Then they seized a bucket and went to see what they could do about Percy's breakfast. Collecting fish from pools was not as easy as the trawling had been. Besides, nearly all the reef fish glittered like living jewels, and it seemed awful to throw them to Percy.

As they moved around the rocky pools, getting nipped by the crabs they gathered, Percy became impatient. He waddled along the beach and climbed up the rocks, no doubt getting hungrier each minute, and anxious to see what his chef was doing about it.

David watched him waddle up behind Danny, who was so absorbed in what she was doing, her ears filled with the whispers and murmurs of the sea, that she didn't remember Percy. He eyed her back as she bent over the pool, lifting a net filled with the glitter of Ali Baba's jewels, and began to throw the lovely little fish back in. Percy gave a clack of disapproval, snaked his long neck forward, and gave her a vigorous nip on her proffered seat! Danny yelled and dropped all the fish, and David laughed so much he lost most of his catch. Percy looked outraged and the children went back to their task.

"I hate feeding Percy live food," Danny sighed. "Why won't he fish for himself?"

Breakfast was a wonderful meal. The air was still comparatively cool, and they cooked eggs and toast on the open fire, sitting where the massed trees backed the

beach and threw their long shadows toward the water. A faint breeze lessened the heat which, as always, seemed to be lying in wait, ready to pounce when the sun rose high enough to flood the world with its hot yellow light.

Percy waddled back from the rocks and stood complainingly behind Danny. Every now and again he tweaked her hair or her shoulder, scolding her in his own way because she was attending to *her* wants instead of rustling up more and yet more food for *his*.

"What are you going to do about that bird?" her mother asked.

"Oh, goodness, I don't know what to do. I want to go with David to the island we saw, but Percy won't let me!"

Her father looked up from where he sat making toast, with the bread on a forked stick held over the coals.

"I think Percy's just a blackmailer," he said. "He could jolly well fish for himself."

"Are you sure he wasn't hurt or anything in the cyclone?"

"Ill? With that appetite!"

"Then why doesn't he fish for himself?"

"Because you're silly enough to do it for him. You go with David—forget Percy. If he looks faint I'll catch him a fish!"

Danny smiled a little shakily. "All right," she said. "Then I will go with David if you're sure he'll be all right."

David broke in with, "May we take the outboard, Dad? It'll take ages to row to the island and it's so hot."

"How far is it?"

"I don't know, perhaps a couple of miles."

"Come on, then, we'll fix the outboard. The men said

it was all right. They put the petrol farther along the beach, just inside that belt of trees. I suppose they thought we'd blow ourselves up if it was next to the camp!"

Mrs. Delaney looked up, saying, "It's a lovely camp. I'm glad they protected it."

Mr. Delaney rose. "Let's go, David. We'll get the outboard rigged up while Danny and your mother tidy up. That's the advantage of being men!"

The big tent in which Mr. and Mrs. Delaney slept also acted as a sitting room. It was a place where the whole family could shelter during rain or storm. Danny began to put the enamel plates together to rinse them in the stream that ran through the trees on the other side of the headland. Percy settled down to sulk, making an occasional sound like the lid of a wooden box closing when Danny went past him. In spite of the size of his beak, it was not very strong. The most he could manage was to tweak a piece of flesh with the very tip of it.

The Delaney women made up the cots, and Danny helped her mother open the canvas chairs and the folding table, take the fronts from the specially built bookcases, and make the lanterns and acetylene lamps ready. When they had finished, the big tent looked very cosy. There were even cushions on the large metal boxes in which spare clothing and bedding were kept. All perishables that the termites might fancy were kept in the boxes, which were proof against all insects and against the moist air. It seemed strange to look out from the comfortably furnished tent to the deserted beach and the empty waters about them and to realize that they were probably the only people within hundreds of miles. The beach was five miles from the shipping lane. Only Captain Morris' knowledge of Reef waters had made it possible for him to land the family and all their gear on the deserted beach.

The sound of an outboard motor came to them, and looking out of the tent flap, they saw Mr. Delaney and David trying out the small outboard on the placid sea.

"Are you leaving Pauli with me, Daniela?"

"Oh, no, Mother, we'll take her. She loves the outboard."

"Percy'll be quite enough to look after. Your father and I are going to spend every day just resting, and don't you and David forget that this holiday is really a convalescence as well."

"We'll remember. Good-bye, Mother. Come on, Pauli." But Pauli was sniffing ecstatically at something that sent her on the trail, like a miniature bloodhound, nose to the ground, in a wobbly line. It led her past Percy, squatting large and white and untidy, with a baleful look in his yellow eyes. Danny turned and called "Pauli!" but Pauli still sniffed the earth, her hindquarters moving in front of Percy. It was a chance not to be resisted. Percy stretched his neck and tweaked her tail.

Pauli yelped and leaped in the air. She forgot whatever she was tracking and pelted off across the sand to where Danny was about to turn around and scold her. When Danny saw her mother laughing and pointing at Percy, she guessed what had happened, and she picked Pauli up and put her in the boat, climbing in after her.

David opened the throttle and the little boat moved off across the water.

Pauli examined her tail inch by inch and decided it was still all there. Because the water was so smooth, the little boat left a wide wake behind it. Danny looked down through the water. It was so clear that even the fading ripples of their movement could not hide the brilliance of the fish below, or the beauty of the growing coral.

Instructed by David, Danny kept a sharp lookout for underwater coral peaks, and they saw something they had missed in their run along the beach the evening before—a tiny coral atoll, covered with the white, moving bodies of seabirds.

As they passed the farther headland and the island came into view, Danny looked up from peering into the water. From the corner of her eye she was sure she saw a movement against the tropical foliage backing the beach.

"I'm sure I saw a man!" she said excitedly. "He disappeared into the bush—look! The leaves are moving!"

"It might be an Abo walking around, but I don't think it was anyone."

"I'm sure it was—I'm sure I saw a man."

"It could have been a cassowary or a kangaroo—or maybe a croc," David added hopefully. He secretly longed to see one of the huge man-eating crocodiles that he knew haunted the Cape York estuaries.

The little boat chugged on and the children forgot all about the incident. The island rose before them, a perfect miniature land, with a thickly wooded hill in the center and beaches and rocky outcrops around the shore. The high top was really what had been the tip of a mainland mountain that had been inundated by the sea millions of years ago. Tiny islands like this one—emerald green and lush—were part of the fascination of the Reef waters and were different from coral atolls, which were bare and hard on the feet.

"We'll go right around it before we decide where to land," David said, turning the boat's nose.

The island was about a mile long and had perfect crescents of beaches on both sides. At one end was a small mangrove swamp, which was dark and smelly, but had an interesting life of its own. At the other end the land flattened in the same way the human instep curves down to the toes. The island's toes were very knobbly, being jumbles of rocks laced by coral now at low tide.

David drove the prow of the little boat up onto the sand and Danny jumped out and took the rope. Pauli leaped out in great excitement and began fussing about, inspecting the place.

"Come on," David called, "but be careful. There could be snakes around—or a croc!"

"You and your crocodiles! Pauli, come here—"

But Pauli was already following jungle trails like the hunter she was, so David and Danny set out after her. They stepped over a hollow in the sand down which flowed a cool, clear little stream of fresh water, and traced it toward the foot of the hill, where a natural hollow formed a sort of basin. Suddenly David stopped and pointed to a piece of soft ground near the pool.

"Look!" he said.

Danny looked and exclaimed excitedly, "Why—that's a horse's hoofmark!"

David nodded. "Yes, it's the hoof of an unshod horse! Now, how on earth—let's look for more."

"Pauli! Pauli!" Danny called. "Come here at once!"

Pauli, as usual, took no notice. Danny peered at the ground with David, and presently they forgot Pauli when they found a tangle of hoofprints on a patch of earth. They tracked them toward the sea until they stood on the edge of the sharp mass of coral leading into the water, where flashes of red and gold and blue darted through the tidal pools. Floating in the shallow water were the fringelike streamers of anemones lying in cinnamon splendor, making Danny feel she must explore the pools.

Both children heard Pauli yelp, but they could not see her. Then came a frightening sound—a snorting and a squealing filled with fury. The tiny brown body of Pauli came racing at desperate speed out of the massed trees, straight toward them.

4

The Siege of Barnacle Bill

Pauli put on a desperate spurt that doubled her long body like a moving caterpillar. She raced from the trees to where the children stood, petrified by the fierce squealing and snorting from the unseen thing coming through the thick undergrowth. Pauli leaped into Danny's arms.

"Get out on the coral—get as far as you can!" David yelled.

His shout sent Danny stumbling out over the sharp, dangerous growth, as a savage, snorting beast broke cover. The big ugly horse came pounding toward them, screaming its rage and snaking its neck. With its ears flattened and its eyes ringed with white, it was as terrifying as only a wild horse can be.

Clutching Pauli under one arm, Danny clung to David's hand with the other. Together they moved to the very far edge of the coral, away from the furious apparition pawing and snorting just along the edge of the sand. David's instinct had been right: the unshod horse would not venture on the terrible cutting combination of coral and rock. With an angry squeal it stamped and pawed. Then, catching sight of a piece of driftwood on which a clutch of barnacles clung, waving their gooselike heads, it stamped and bit it to shreds.

"Golly!" David breathed. "That's a savage brute, all right! He's a real old Barnacle Bill!"

"Did you notice all the scars on his hide?"

"Yes, frightful ones on his rump and down his neck and near his shoulder. He's got two awful spur-scar patches on his sides, too. He must have been ridden by a brute of a man." Danny suddenly saw a look of alarm on David's face as he added, "I hope he won't see the outboard and smash it up!"

"How are we going to get to it?"

Where they stood the rocks and the coral made a long tongue out into the sea. They were marooned. It wasn't possible to guess how long the horse would keep them in a state of siege as he marched up and down. Each moment increased the risk of his seeing the outboard on the beach. Every time they went toward the horse they were met by a display of rearing, savagely beating hooves, so they retreated within the safety margin of rough coral.

"Look, Danny!" David said abruptly. "Something else is coming out of the bushes—look at the leaves rustling."

They looked beyond the powerful enemy confronting them and saw what seemed like a vision from fairyland. Two more horses, as nervously beautiful as unicorns on their way to drink, stepped warily through the dark green of the leaves of the slender, silver-barked trees. Obviously much younger than the scarred old brown horse, the shapely creatures had beautiful thoroughbred heads, slender legs, and hooves that badly needed trimming. They stood motionless, heads raised, nostrils wide, their intelligent eyes on the children, but their eyes were not rimmed with the white of fear and anger as were the eyes of the old warrior horse.

"They're lovely!" Danny breathed softly.

"Golly! they *are* beauts!" David declared.

The stallion was black with a pale silvery belly, unlike anything the children had seen before. The mare was delicately lovely, her hide a dappled silvery gray. She seemed to be created from moonlight as she stood in quivering stillness against the dark background.

"I wonder who owns them and why he isn't here."

"No one owns them," David said impatiently. "Look at the condition of their hooves."

"Yet Old Barnacle Bill's hooves aren't too bad."

"He's getting old—the young one's hooves are softer and they grow faster."

"Oh, David, I wish they belonged to us!"

David turned and looked at his sister curiously. "Why shouldn't they?" he asked.

"But we'll never get near them with Old Bill ramping and roaring there."

David looked at her oddly and said, "I'll bet you could tame him, given the time, and we *have* the time!"

"Wouldn't that be wonderful? I wonder what Dad would say."

"We won't tell him anything about them until they're all tamed!"

Danny looked about her. She had almost forgotten that they were marooned on the coral in her interest in what David was saying. Now she looked at the big horse. He was eyeing them balefully and the boat could still be smashed by his punishing hooves. The whole project of taming the horses seemed a very long way away. Still, she wasn't going to say so to David. He would only get a superior look on his face and tell her she was behaving like a girl, and this obvious fact was, to both of them, the worst insult he could offer her. So she merely said, "All right, we can try and tame them. But right now, how are we ever going to get off these rocks? We can't explore the island because of that naughty old Barnacle Bill."

"Poor old Barnacle Bill. He's been badly knocked about. Those wounds might be from sharks or even a crocodile."

Danny glanced fiercely at David, and her freckled face screwed itself into an angry frown. "Those two spur patches must have been done by a human," she said. "I'd like to make him trust me if it's only to prove that all humans aren't like whoever did that to him."

Pauli was getting very heavy on Danny's arm and she looked around for somewhere to sit down, but at the slightest movement the brown horse began to snake his neck and paw the ground.

"You silly thing!" Danny told him. "We wouldn't hurt you for anything."

Danny found a patch of rock that wasn't much of a seat but was better than standing. She dared not put Pauli down to cut her fat paws on the coral.

"I guess all we can do, David, is to hope that Barnacle Bill gets hungry before we starve."

David didn't answer. He looked around and walked away to the left and then across the rocks in the opposite direction. The horse snorted, keeping parallel with him. David returned to Danny.

"I think I'll swim around and try to get the boat off the beach without Old Bill's catching me," said David.

Danny wasn't listening, for she was watching the other two horses and saying, "They look like thoroughbreds. I'll bet they've been well-handled. I wonder how they got here."

"Never mind the horses—listen to me, Danny. I said I'd swim around and bring the boat for you, if I don't hole her on the coral first."

"But David, we don't know these waters. What about sharks?"

David shrugged. "I'll have to chance it. I suppose

there are sharks everywhere, but now it's about midday and not so bad as at sundown when they start feeding."

Danny looked doubtful, but David brushed all her objections aside. "You shuffle yourself over to that side and

Old Bill will follow you. Keep his attention when I get to the boat. I'll slip off the end there and you make him watch you. I don't want him charging down on me before I can get the boat out."

"Oh, dear, I wish we didn't have to do it this way," Danny said unhappily, but David laughed at her and began to make his way across the rocks. Instantly the big horse was alert and angry. The two young horses lifted their heads and then, as if used to the spectacle of Old Bill challenging the world, they went on picking grass.

None of the horses was fat and obviously food was not very plentiful.

Danny watched David making his way to the edge of the rocky peninsula. Then she attracted Old Bill's attention by walking in the other direction. David disappeared into the sea, and there were no further sounds except for an occasional indignant snort from Old Bill or a grumble from Pauli, who was tired of being carried.

David slid into the water and pushed himself off from the deadly cutting coral. The water was so clear that for a moment he felt as if he were suspended in the air and might at any moment go bump on the floor of the sea below him. He saw myriad tiny brilliant fish weaving their way among clams and anemones. Below him a long silvery-dark fish slid by, and he thought that it was probably a barracuda and remembered how divers say they would rather face a shark any day than those wolves of the sea. Sharks swim around a man and give him warning if they are going to attack, but barracuda close in. This one did not seem interested and David swam on, neither hurrying nor splashing, seeing what he could of the world about him. It wasn't far to where the boat rocked gently, half in the water, its prow on the sand and the rope looped onto a stick. He lowered his feet cautiously and waded toward the boat. If the big horse charged now, it would be the end of the outboard. Even if he got the boat off, there was still a chance that the horse would plunge into the water after it.

Danny talked continuously to Old Bill, and when he seemed to be losing interest she threw a loose piece of coral toward him. Each throw sent him into a fresh paroxysm of rage and kept him from going over the rise to see David pushing the outboard off the beach.

At last she heard the put-putting of the motor. Old Bill heard it too and charged off toward the strange noise. The two grazing youngsters lifted their heads, amazed at Bill's excitement, and went back to feeding. Soon Danny saw the little boat coming around the rocks. Once aboard, both children felt loath to leave, but there seemed nothing else to do.

"D'you know what *I* think?" Danny asked. "I think that half that nonsense with Old Bill is just bluff and the other half is fear. If we can show him we're his friends we'll be halfway there. D'you think we could find sweet grass on the mainland and gather some for the three horses?"

"Why not! It's a good idea. We'll look for it, but don't say anything to Dad."

As they turned and chugged toward their home beach Danny called out to David, "There! What did I tell you?"

David turned his head and gave a whistle of surprise. "You really did see someone this morning."

As he peered at the motionless figure on the headland a second man appeared. It was too far away to see their faces. The men stood there without waving, so, obviously, they did not want to know their neighbors. David opened the throttle and the boat gathered speed. Danny glanced down and gripped the sides of the boat.

"It's not like water at all down there," she said in a startled voice. "It's so clear I feel as if the boat might drop through it. Oh, there's a big shark, isn't it? No, it's a grouper—I can see its huge mouth!"

"They say their mouths can be big enough to swallow a man, so it wouldn't be much better than being eaten by a shark. I noticed how the water looked like air when I was swimming for the boat. I expect it's the time of day —the light's going straight down. Someday we'll come out and just drift around looking into the water."

Danny peered into the water. "It's beautiful— just like a garden of living flowers! Down there I can see a tiny brilliant blue fish, and yellow ones, and one that's bright scarlet with lovely fluttery fins like wings."

"That's probably a fire-fish. Dad says they give you a terrible sting if you brush against them. Come on, don't forget, not a word to Mother or Dad until we're riding the horses all over the island!"

Danny laughed. "You *are* ambitious! I'll be satisfied if Old Barnacle Bill lets us *walk* all over the island! And I bet you he will, and pretty soon now, too."

Before them swept the lovely curve of the home beach, shining in the golden noonday sun. "I wonder how Percy's behaving himself," Danny remarked anxiously.

"Oh, Dad'll look after Percy. He's probably fishing right alongside Dad now, but I'll bet he'll stop and lie back when he sees you. Percy knows a mug when he sees one!"

Mr. Delaney rose from one of the long canvas chairs

in the shade of the big tent and Mrs. Delaney waved from the other chair. The children brought the boat up on the sand.

"Have a good morning?" their father shouted.

"Fine!"

"How was the island?"

"It's beautiful," David assured him, looking warningly at Danny. "You and Mother must see it when you're feeling better."

Pauli galloped ahead, threw herself in the shade, and promptly went to sleep. Danny looked around for Percy.

"Where's Percy?" she asked. "Was he a nuisance?"

"Percy! You wait till I tell you about that Percy!"

"But he's all right, isn't he?" Danny asked anxiously.

Her father gave her an outraged look. "All right!" he repeated. "Well, if he's not, he ought to be. Just wait until I tell you about that wicked old sinner!"

5

Percy Calls It a Day

That day they had lunch in the comparative coolness of the tent. Danny poured a long drink from a canvas water-bag hanging from the tent pole. Evaporation had cooled the water, but the bag, being made of new canvas, made the water taste musty. She made a face as she hung the enameled mug back on the wire hook.

"Come on, Danny, let's have lunch."

"What've we got, Mother?"

"We still have some of the ship's food. It's kept fresh very well."

"Sit down, you kids, and I'll tell you why we're *not* having lovely fresh fish for lunch!"

Danny sat down. "Oh, dear, was it Percy?"

"It was indeed. Having lost his slave, he decided to re-sort to robbery with violence!"

"Poor old Percy, what did he do?"

"Poor old Percy? Poor old Dad! I set off to catch our dinner and Percy waddled after me. He wouldn't fly, oh, no. He just wobbled along, clacking his beak, and I reached the headland long before he showed up. I began to fish—it was marvelous. I was pulling them in by the

45

dozen, taking the best for us, and being decent enough to put the spares in a little pool beside me for Percy. Along he came at last and I showed him his pool. He looked in it, then sat back and waited for me to feed him, which I was silly enough to do—"

"You see!" Danny broke in triumphantly. "He's not a bit easy to refuse."

"Hmm, I suppose we must just be feebleminded as a family. Anyway, I emptied his pool and then went back to my fishing. Perhaps I'd been fishing a shoal and they'd left, but whatever it was, the fish stopped biting. Then a snapper or something bit my line through and went off with the hook. I was so busy with that that I didn't look at Percy again until I'd wound up my line and decided to call it a day. I turned around to pick up my fish bucket and it was empty. Percy squatted there, his beak packed with fish and an insolent look in his eye!"

"Oh, Dad, you didn't frighten him?"

"What do you think I am?" her father said indignantly. "I left him to sleep it off."

"I'll go and look for him when we finish lunch."

"Now you two," Mrs. Delaney said firmly, "you must rest for at least an hour."

"But I have to find Percy first."

Mr. Delaney turned to David. "I think you could take the dinghy and leave it on the mainland beach somewhere opposite your island. Then you can ferry yourselves back and forth and be independent if your mother and I want the outboard."

"Oh, that'd be great, Dad. It doesn't take long to walk to the far beach—it's much easier than rowing."

His father nodded. "We don't much feel like using the outboard yet awhile and there's plenty to do around camp."

"I'll help you clear up, Mother."

"Hold on a minute, Danny. I want David to help me move his tent right beside yours. It's not that there's anything—" her father finished lamely. The children looked at him round-eyed and he went on. "It's only that there are lots of—well, creatures moving on the beach at night, you know—wild cats, possums, that sort of thing. They might disturb you, Danny."

"Oh, I'm not afraid of any animals."

"No, of course not, but I'd be happier if I knew you could call out and that David was near to see what was up."

"Pauli would soon wake me if anything came around."

"Anyhow, we'll move that tent. And, David, you take one of the guns into your tent—you never know."

The children glanced at each other, but they asked no questions. Danny set about helping her mother while David and his father moved the tent. Danny was looking for Percy when she heard David calling her. She slipped out of the tent and Pauli woke and galloped after her. David was standing near the creek. There, on the slightly soft ground, were tracks that were strange to Danny— big handlike tracks. She looked at David.

"Those are croc tracks," he said.

"So that's why Dad wants our tents together and you're to have the gun and everything!"

David nodded. "It must have been here last night. I suppose Dad saw other tracks and brushed them away this morning in case they worried Mother."

Danny squatted on her heels and looked at the big marks. "Well, I hope it doesn't come around again. Now I have to go and find Percy."

Danny went first to the rock pools, but there was no sign of the big white bird there or on the beach. She went back to the tent and told her father.

"I can't find Percy," she said. "You don't think he's flown away, do you?"

"He might have. Come on, I'll look too."

Halfway to the beach Mr. Delaney stopped and shaded his eyes with his hand. Danny copied him. There, very high up in the blue sky over the sea, hovered a tiny silvery-white speck.

"I wonder if that could be Percy."

The bright speck floated high in the air, then planed down on the air currents and balanced on spread wings, its eyes peering into the sea. Across the calm water a shoal of small silvery fish rose like the arch of a rainbow, drops glittering from their bodies and spattering on the water below. The bright speck grew larger. It was a big black and white bird, and they thought it must be Percy.

"Don't move—let's see what he's going to do."

Percy, so grotesque on land, so lovely in the air, looked like some splendid white galleon.

"I once saw about a dozen pelicans swept past me by a cyclone," Mr. Delaney told Danny. "They were out of control because the wind got into their pouches and ballooned them out like little sails."

Percy rode high in the air, hovering above the shoal of

small fish. Then the big pelican dropped like a stone. He landed on the calm water a little distance from the shoal and began to churn the surface with his great wings.

"What's he doing?" Danny asked.

"He's on the seaward side. I think he's chasing the shoal into the shallows."

"Like a sheepdog yarding sheep."

When the fish tried to break past him Percy paddled frantically and churned the water into froth again. Presently the fish were in the shallow water, with Percy strutting among the panicky things, eating his fill.

"What a clever boy!" Danny said fondly.

"Yes, and you be a clever girl and let him get on with it. Don't begin feeding him again, at least not completely, or he'll return to being an old layabout."

Percy waddled back and made a bulge in the side of Danny's tent, and the whole family, including Pauli, slept soundly. Later they all went for a swim, wearing their frogmen's flippers and masks and using their snorkels.

Underwater it was unbelievably beautiful. They swam slowly through corridors walled by coral reefs, through a silent garden as lovely as any on earth. A tiny scarlet firefish threaded its way around a royal-blue angelfish, a little yellow fish, and a baby angelfish, which was white with transverse stripes of deep blue. All flitted about like butterflies.

Diving deeply, they saw coral in all its beauty; the warmth of the water brought a rainbow gathering of tiny fish, and the depth expanded the coral polyps into bouquets of color, turning this garden of the sea into one of ravishing beauty. The only large fish they saw were a school of mullet browsing on seaweed.

They left the water and lay on the sand on their towels, watching the blue-gray elegance of the reef herons on the nearest headland. Mr. Delaney rolled his towel and put it under his head and gazed up at his children.

"I believe you two look better already," he said.

"Oh, they do!" Mrs. Delaney assured him.

"Maybe it's the coral we've just visited," he went on.

"The Romans used to hang branches of it around their children's necks as a sort of cure-all. They say there's black coral on the Reef—the kind they find in the Persian Gulf. We must watch for it."

"When I was a child," Danny began, with a weary air that made everyone laugh at her, "our governess used to tell us that coral was made by insects."

"You can forget that piece of misinformation," her father told her. "Coral is formed by animals no bigger than the head of a pin, and, what's more, they only eat animal foods."

"It must take an awful lot of them an awful lot of time to build a reef!"

"It takes billions of animals billions of years. The best coral needs the drive of seawater against it—that's why the outer reef is the biggest. Coral babies are pear-shaped specks covered with tiny hairs, which they use like oars. They might swim around for weeks, then settle on a hard surface when they've developed into a cup shape. Then they build themselves up from the lime they extract from seawater."

They all dozed for a few minutes. Then Pauli scratched sand over David's face and he woke Danny, saying it was time for a walk.

"Where are you going?" Mr. Delaney asked sleepily.

"Oh, along the beaches toward the island, and we'll take a look at the bush behind the beaches too."

"All right, don't go too far, and watch out for snakes or crocodiles."

"We will. We won't wake Mother. Danny, put on your

thick sandals and dungarees—the bush'll be scratchy."

The children passed the first headland and found the bush backing the beach so thick that they were some time finding an opening. They entered a dim world of green light, so that it was like walking under water. It was tiring walking in a world of growing, twisting, thorny things, and David was just about to say, "We'll never find any grass here," when it thinned out and roundish gaps appeared. Where the sunlight could reach the earth, the grass grew.

"It won't be easy to pick much of it. We'll bring one of those canvas bags and stop the outboard opposite. Let's go a bit farther into the thick jungle."

Although the children lived in Brisbane, they had spent most of their lives in the bush, and they walked silently as bushmen do. Winding through the undergrowth, they now and again came on what seemed like narrow tunnels, obviously made by some animal.

They were going to step into one of these when David, who was leading, stopped and pressed back against Danny. She lifted Pauli to keep her quiet. Something was coming along the tunnel through the green gloom. Silently the two children pushed themselves to one side so that they were partly hidden by bushes.

There was the faint, muffled thud of feet, more a vibration of the earth than an actual step, and along the tunnel toward them came a great black cassowary. It towered over their heads, and in the half-light its feathers shone glossily black. It was far more thickset than an emu, with colored wattles and that strange casque, like a

Roman helmet, growing on its head. Both children knew that cassowaries are pugnacious and will attack man if annoyed, biting and kicking just like a horse.

Danny clutched Pauli, who wriggled but fortunately didn't bark. The cassowary came nearer, towering over

the two, who were trying to efface themselves in the shadows. They looked with awe at the powerful feet and legs of the big bird.

It was just too much for Pauli, who gave a series of high-pitched yelps. The cassowary stopped dead. In the gloom it looked as big as a door, though it was probably only a few inches over five feet. It turned its head, saw nothing, turned right around, and then disappeared along the tunnel.

Silently the children pushed through the undergrowth, breathing sighs of relief when they emerged onto the beach and into the sunlight. No cassowary would find them there, for the big birds dislike light and lurk only in the shadows.

After dinner they sprawled on the beach, where tiny waves lapped the sand with their silvered edges of cold fire. Whenever a fish jumped, it left the water in the same silver blaze of phosphorus. Around them small bats flitted like imps of the night. They all turned in early.

"Give a shout if anything disturbs you," David said to Danny.

Danny laughed and hugged Pauli. "Don't worry— nothing disturbs Pauli and me."

6

A Stranger in the Night

*O*utside the net the mosquitoes zoomed around, making a high whining noise like someone continuously playing on one string of a tiny violin. Inside the net Danny slept, tired after her long day, too tired to notice that Pauli was burrowed into her back like a fat, hot little poultice.

A cube of brilliant moonlight shone through the tent flap and fell on the earthen floor. Now David and Danny had almost adjoining "front doors" and Percy made his usual bulge at the end of the tent.

It was very quiet and still in the bush outside, and the children were so tired that the dragging sound coming toward the tents did not disturb them, and Pauli slept on, too. The dragging stopped. Silently the long snout and cold eyes of a crocodile inched through the open flap. The long body stretching back into the moonlight reflected a peculiar frosty light from the moon, as though a white scum lay on the dark scales.

The crocodile paused. It turned its head and looked about the tiny tent, obviously puzzled by the strange object covered in the white folds of the mosquito net. Then perhaps the delicious smell of its favorite food, dog, came through the humid air. The long sinister head stretched out, the great beast raised its fifteen-foot length on crooked legs, preparing to rush its victims, and as it did so it brought its jaws together with a quick snap.

Instantly Pauli lifted her own long-snouted head and gave a shrill yap, uncurling her pliant body and leaping onto Danny's side as she turned to face the terrible marauder. The crocodile's rush was halted and it swayed on its clawed feet.

David, wakened by the wild yap, leaped from his bed, seized the gun, and ran to the flap of his tent. As Danny sat up clutching Pauli, David saw the scaly length before him, its head cut off by Danny's tent. He fired at random —anything to stop the deadly rush.

The crack of the rifle startled the half-awake Danny. She held Pauli firmly and stared with terrified eyes at the cruel head, and heard the thud of the bullet on the creature's armored side. It did not penetrate the scales, but the impact of the bullet jerked the crocodile's body and stopped its rush. Instantly it dropped low to the ground and swung its head, and the tail scythed around with the turning body as it backed out.

David knew that he must wait for the head to appear. The only chance was to aim at the eye or the less armored part of the body behind the front legs. It was terrible standing helplessly there. A light went on in his parents' tent and his father shouted to him. In an instant that seemed like an eternity he realized that he must get the crocodile in one shot or it would either rush at Danny or charge him. Pauli still barked hysterically.

The long terrible head followed the turning body and the tiny eyes gleamed in the moonlight. Steadying himself against an upright, David fired. The great crocodile roared and its body rose in an arc. David knew that he

had won. As it thrashed about on the ground Mr. Delaney came running out with his gun, his wife following him. The whole thing had been terribly quick, a couple of minutes in all, and now David felt rather shaken. The brute had so nearly got Danny and Pauli—he couldn't bear to think what would have happened if he had missed.

The beast's movements stopped. The whole family stood there, Danny in pajamas and still holding Pauli, David white-faced, busying himself with removing the used cartridge with hands that shook a little, their parents silent before the thought of the terrible danger from which their children had escaped. The crocodile rolled over and lay quiet. Mrs. Delaney put her arms around Danny, and Mr. Delaney's hand was on David's shoulder as he said, "Well done, son."

David turned to his father and said, with a shaky smile, "Can we have coffee in your tent and leave this— mess for a while?"

Everyone's spirits revived as they sat together, safe in the soft yellow lamplight, with David chuckling as Danny reminded him how often he had said he wanted to see one of the man-eaters of the estuaries!

"Keep hold of Pauli, Danny," Mr. Delaney said. "Crocs are cold-blooded—sometimes they can move for an hour or more after they've been shot. Poor devil, I wish it had minded its own business, but I'm afraid that after it got wind of Pauli it would keep coming back— crocs love dog flesh."

Danny bent down and snuggled Pauli, who was most astonished at the whole thing and quite willing to go out and challenge the crocodile herself. Only then did someone remember that Percy had slept through the entire affair.

"Would you like to finish the night here?"

"Oh no, Mother! We got a fright, but it's over now."

"We'll skin it later, David."

"Oh yes—it must be sixteen or seventeen feet."

"Well, say fifteen, and that's pretty big. Anyway, it's your skin, son, if we can get it off!"

Mr. Delaney walked over to their tents with them, avoiding the big moonlight-silvered heap before Danny's tent.

Soon after daylight the skinning began. It was hard work. Once off, the inside of the skin had to be scraped, washed, and rubbed with salt. Knowing they might want to preserve specimens of some kind, Mr. Delaney had had a barrel of salt landed from the *Captain Cook,* and forty pounds of it was rubbed into the long skin. Between them, David and his father dragged the salted skin and draped it over a fallen tree. The salt would keep it safe from dingoes and wild cats as well as from insects. That still left the great carcass to be disposed of. Mr. Delaney decided they'd chop it up and bury it well away from the tents.

It was after eleven when the job was finished, and David suggested that he and Danny take a picnic lunch and tow the dinghy behind the outboard, finally leaving it on the beach on their way home. Both children were tired but determined to cut grass for the horses and to begin the taming process.

"What's the sack for?" Mr. Delaney inquired.

"Oh—we might pick up something."

David threw in their underwater gear, fastened the dinghy to the outboard, and ordered his crew aboard. The hot sun made them all drowsy, even Pauli. High in the sky hovered a little silvery mothlike thing that Danny was sure must be Percy, who, after failing to bully Danny into working for him, had taken off to fish for himself.

They chugged all around the headland and stopped opposite yesterday's grassy patches. It was really hard work filling the sacks with grass, and then the island was to be the next step. They decided to put the grass bag in the dinghy, leaving the outboard on the mainland beach, and to try and land quietly on the island before Barnacle Bill thundered down from the mountain.

There was no sign of the horses as they approached the little beach. "We'll tip it out here, on this flat patch, and then get back in the dinghy and make a noise."

They upended the bag, and the grass fell in a heap on the ground. "I hope the wind doesn't rise and blow it about," Danny said nervously.

David ran toward the rocks and picked up a few big chunks. "These ought to bring Old Barnacle if we throw them hard at the rocks over there," he said.

Shouting and calling "Kip, kip!" they threw the rocks onto the coral. A wild screaming neigh rewarded them as they retreated to the dinghy. Before they had time to push Pauli into the little boat they could hear a crashing among the trees. They jumped in and picked up the oars and put a strip of water between themselves and the island. Old Bill came charging out of the thick growth, making a half-neighing sound and shaking his head. The other two followed him.

"Oh, don't they look lovely!" Danny said breathlessly. "I'd love the gray mare, David. I'd call her Cloud, because she looks just like those dappled clouds you sometimes see in the sky."

David nodded. "The black one'll do me," he said. "I've never seen a horse with an almost white stomach before. I know, I'll call him Manta—he's just like one of those rays we saw jumping when we were on the *Captain Cook:* black on top, white underneath."

"Poor Old Bill, neither of us asked for him."

"Well, we'll share him, if he'll let us. Look at the old monkey—he's beginning to sniff at the grass."

Old Bill sniffed and pawed; then, lifting his head, he looked at the children and gave his squealing neigh. After that he began eating the grass ravenously. The two beautiful beasts behind him came nearer, hesitated, and joined in.

"Oh, I'm sure that'll tame them, if we can only get enough of it!" Danny exclaimed.

As they watched, the three horses cleaned up every blade of grass, and the children wished they had been able to bring twice as much.

"Let's throw out the anchor and swim."

"What about the sharks?" asked Danny.

David shrugged. "Sharks could be anywhere," he said, "but if we're underwater it'll be all right. Dad says it's surface swimming that's dangerous—you can't see what's coming at you. Anyway, splashing on top of the water is what attracts them. I'll go down and let you know if all's clear."

After a couple of minutes David reappeared.

"The coral isn't as good as it is in the deep water, but there's plenty of it, and I've something to show you, so hurry up."

Danny swam lazily after David and he led her to where the reef stretched before them like a stone wall. One end had crumbled—some of the coral was dead and had turned black—but most of the wall at the other end was full of tiny fishy faces peering at them. One hole had a greasy black edge that puzzled Danny. They surfaced, got their breath, and went down again. Now the greasy hole was filled with the strangest face Danny had ever seen. It was a chocolate color, the big mouth opened and closed all the time, and the body was invisible. Big teeth filled the gaping mouth, and as she watched, the whole face contorted in the most extraordinary way.

The children shot to the surface.

"What do you think of that?" David asked, grinning at her.

"What is it?"

"That was a moray eel. Dad showed me one a long time ago. It was trying to frighten us away from its hole by making faces at us."

"Goodness, will they bite too?" Danny asked.

"Not if you don't interfere with their homes. Dad said the Romans kept them as pets and trained them to come when they were called and dressed them up with earrings! They open and shut their mouths to drive the water through their gills to extract the oxygen. It makes them look awfully ferocious."

"I'd hate to see one on a dark night."

"I wouldn't like a bite from one either. They say if you put your hand near their holes, they grab it and hang on, swelling their necks so you can't pull it out. Morays have poison sacs, but the poison isn't very severe."

"Let's row around the island and have a look at the mangrove swamp."

As they climbed, dripping, into the dinghy, Pauli rose with great dignity and moved away, for she was not amused by such behavior. In fact she was feeling rather annoyed, what with the disturbing night she had suffered and now having water dripped all over her. She curled up disgustedly on the floorboards, ignoring everyone, and went to sleep.

The mangrove swamp gave out its own peculiar odor, a rather unpleasant rotting smell. The children peered through the entwined roots, but it was too dense to force the dinghy through it. Among all the black roots that looked like crazy plumbing, David and Danny knew, lay a little isolated world—a world with creatures that had learned to live on mud. Whelks crawled over it; oysters fastened themselves to the mangrove roots; worms, crabs, and fish lived in the muddy darkness. But most curious of all was the mudskipper.

These little oddities are about a foot long, brownish with pale spots, and look like miniature seals with frog's faces. Their breast fins are shaped for walking on the mud or for helping them climb the mangroves for a foot or two. Mudskippers drown if kept too long in water, and when they are not skipping across the mud or basking on mangrove limbs, they sit with the tips of their tails in the water, which helps them breathe by carrying oxygen into their blood.

Danny pulled the black mangrove boughs apart and looked about her. Suddenly she saw a mudskipper crossing a tiny open space. She called David to look. It walked in short jerks, but when in her excitement she let a bough fly back, the mudskipper, frightened, curled its tail sideways and gave a flick with it, which propelled the little creature three feet toward its next perch.

"If we ever explore this properly, it'll have to be from land," David said, pushing the little dinghy backward.

"Then it'll depend on the horses," Danny said with a sigh. "I think we'll have to work harder on this holiday than we ever have at home."

She was quite right. Every day after that the children made a frantic search for grass. As a reward for all their efforts, in less than a week they could tell that Old Bill, as well as the others, looked forward to his daily treat.

"Tomorrow, Danny," said David, "we're going to land on that island and make friends with the horses, and Old Bill's going to have to like it—or else!"

7

The Beachcombers

We shouldn't have brought Pauli," Danny said as she and David trudged along the beach, lugging the bagful of grass.

"Oh, why not? The horses'll have to get used to her too. Dad would have wondered if we'd left her behind. It was bad enough, anyway," he added gloomily, thinking of how his father had said, "I might come along with you kids this afternoon and take a look at your island." Fortunately their mother broke in and told him severely he'd do nothing of the sort.

Danny chuckled, slogging her feet through the sand. "Good old Mother!" she said. "It was touch and go before she began to fuss!"

They dumped the grass-filled sack near the edge of the water and walked back up the track the dinghy had made when they had pulled it into the undergrowth.

"It looks like a turtle track," Danny said. Pauli sniffed at the wide furrow and ran up it in a frightfully clever way, as if she expected to find some strange beast at the end of it.

They began pulling the dinghy back into the sand to push it down the slope to the water. Both children leaned forward, grunting and shoving, when Pauli, who was sniffing around the edge of the bush, gave a sharp yelp.

"I wonder what she's found." Danny stopped pushing and straightened up. She mopped her dripping forehead.

Pauli yelped again and David said, "She's probably cornered a lizard. Come on, do some work."

Danny gripped the edge of the dinghy, and Pauli yelped again. Danny let go saying, "David, it might be a snake. I think we ought to go and look."

"Oh, never mind the little monkey! All right, all right, we're coming," he shouted to the impatient Pauli.

They pushed their way into the bush to where they saw her scratching and sniffing and peering at the ground. There on the soft earth were the marks of naked human feet. Someone had inspected the dinghy. Instantly they both thought of the two men they had seen on the first day. They looked at each other.

"I wonder what they wanted."

"Curiosity, I suppose. They didn't take it."

"Oh, well, it doesn't matter, but you'd think, seeing how far we are away from other people, they'd want to say hello to us, wouldn't you?"

Danny nodded and they both returned to pushing the dinghy down to the water, throwing the sack in and jumping in themselves. David rowed and Danny was glad to sit back and trail her fingers through the cool water. She took her turn and was rowing when David told her to stop and look toward the island. She turned and saw the three horses standing on the beach, obviously sure that the little boat was bringing them a treat.

The two young horses trotted up and down, making soft whinnying noises of welcome. Old Barnacle Bill, the die-hard type, pawed halfheartedly at the ground and endeavored to snake his neck, but it was obvious that his heart wasn't in it. There was an element of uncertainty in attempting to land, for possibly Old Bill might turn nasty, but they had to take a chance.

"We'll leave the dinghy anchored a little way out with Pauli in it, and wade in ourselves."

"Anyway, if we can land the grass and bring the bag back, that'll be a real step forward," Danny said.

The horses wove themselves into a moving pattern as the children dropped the anchor and got out of the boat. David shouldered the sack.

"David, let me go first."

"All right, but be careful, Danny."

Danny walked quietly just ahead of David. The two young horses retreated, but Old Bill held his ground, curled his top lip, and put his ears back. Danny walked right up to that wicked head, saying, "Go on, you old fraud!" and put her hand up, calmly rubbing the astonished Bill's forehead. If a horse's jaw could be said to drop, then Old Bill's did. Here he was, Old Bill, the terror of the island, and a chit of a girl was treating him like this!

David had seen Danny's magic with animals at work too often to be very astonished now, but he was a little nervous for her. He breathed a sigh of relief when the flattened ears, the bared teeth, and the snakelike head became normal. Still rubbing Old Bill's ears, Danny said, "Give me some grass," and held her left hand out behind her. David did as he was told and Danny tickled

Bill's nose with it. He clamped his strong yellow teeth over it and began to chew, wearing such a blissful look that Danny slipped her arms around his neck while he stood chewing like an old cart horse.

But when Bill's snack was gone and Danny and David tried to tilt the grass onto the ground, it was another matter. The three horses rushed it, and the children had to snatch the sack away and shake it out a few feet from them, while the horses ate the first heap down to the last grass blade.

David was proud of his sister. "Good for you, Danny! You really did have the old fellow eating out of your hand!"

"Well, it's a beginning, but we'll have to work jolly hard on all three of them before we can let Dad see them, and that'll mean cutting an awful lot more grass!"

"Never mind, as long as we can bring it and stay around the island, I think they'll tame pretty quickly. They're not like horses that have never been handled."

"I tried to pat Cloud when she was eating, but she dodged away. Still, we've really started. I hope they won't be silly about meeting Pauli. What'll we do now?"

"Stick around awhile and see if the horses'll let us get near them. Anyway, they'll get a little used to us."

But once the grass was gone, the horses became elusive. Old Bill, though he ceased to give his impression of an evil horse, still shook his head and pawed the ground a little when either of the children went near him. The young horses moved about restlessly, looking at them with wide, shy eyes, and they finally disappeared up the steep side of the hill.

"I guess we ought to push off and have a look around the next headland."

"Then we could have a swim on the way home."

"Yes, let's do that. Come on then."

They waded out to the dinghy, and Old Bill watched them go, tossing his head as much as to say *he* didn't care. They felt that he would really like them to stay if only to be an audience for his fierce-horse act.

Danny was pleased with their day's work. It left her with an affectionate feeling for Old Bill, but David felt something more. He had been brought up among horses and he knew that without Danny's own peculiar personal magic Old Bill might have remained forever the killer he undoubtedly was, or at best he would be only partially tameable. David never said much to Danny about her special gift. He had a feeling it was something she *was*, and that the less she thought about *why* she was like that the better it would be. Often David wondered, and worried too, that it might leave her when she grew up, but he did not really believe it would.

David rowed toward the beach, and Danny leaned back, quiet and dreamy as she often was after she had been establishing a friendship with some animal, as though some part of herself had been drained away and needed time to renew itself.

In twenty minutes Danny was her usual lively self again, and Pauli, glad to be on dry land, dashed around with a stick in her mouth, rushing past the children and swiping their legs with the leafy end, filled with glee when she made them jump.

So far all the beaches they had seen had ended in rocky headlands, and this one was no exception. They reached the far rocks and paused to look into a small pool. It had a smooth, sandy floor, only just covered by water. The sand had been swept in by the tides of hundreds, perhaps thousands, of years until it covered the rocky basin to a depth of several inches. A few small fish flitted about, but what fascinated the children was a sandy blister, about as big as a dinner plate, rising in the center of the pool. They knew that this raised circle was made by a stingray, which had burrowed beneath the sand.

The children avoided walking through the pool, treating it with great respect. They knew about the terrible barb on a stingray's tail and the agonizing poison it injects. The barb of a big stingray is so sharp and hard that Aboriginals bind them to the tips of their hunting spears. The other pools had much kinder denizens, principally *bêche-de-mer*. On the whole Danny thought them ugly creatures, like sausages, with dark brown or black skins. Sometimes feathery tentacles showed at the mouth, where the creatures took in mud, gravel, or sand, just whatever happened to be there.

"Dad calls them sea cucumbers. People used to smoke them and sell them to the Chinese for soup or something. They call them trepang. Rich Chinese liked the red ones that you don't find on the Reef, so the men used to boil the black ones with the roots of the mangroves, and they turned red. That way they sold for more."

"Well, I just think they're ugly and I'd hate to eat any of them. Oh, here's the beach. Isn't it pretty with that big coral tree growing at the other end?"

They stood balanced on a rock and looked across the quarter-moon curve of the beach. It was smaller than their own camping beach.

"Oh, look—there's something under that coral tree— it looks like the ashes of a fire."

"Let's go and take a look."

They scrambled down off the rocks, and, with Pauli racing ahead, they followed the curve of the small lapping waves toward the coral tree, one of the biggest of the trees that grow on Australian beaches, and which sends out long roots to extract limestone from the sand. The trunk of this one could have been fifteen feet around and the huge roots made snakelike coils beneath the sand.

They stood looking down at the warm ashes of the fire. When Pauli began to bark they glanced up and saw two men coming from the wall of green behind them. The children called out a polite "Hello," and the men growled something that didn't sound half as polite. Bristling a little and barking, Pauli stood between the men and what was obviously their fire.

One of them, a sullen, dark-faced man said, "Git out yer mongrel. Git out or I'll kick yer."

Danny was furious, but as long as David stood his ground she would stand beside him. She called Pauli to her, and for once she came without argument.

"I suppose this is your camp," said David, ignoring the ill-tempered man. "Ours is three beaches back."

In a heavy foreign accent the second man, who had fair hair and a bloated red face, said, "None of your business."

David looked them coolly up and down and Danny felt proud of him. She herself was boiling with rage because Pauli had been threatened and called a mongrel, but she wisely decided to let David handle the situation.

David waited a moment, then he said quietly, "I thought we were the only people on this part of the coast and that you might like to know who we are, but it really doesn't matter to us. Come on, Danny."

He turned his back and walked along the hard sand and Danny and Pauli ran after him. David had really won all the honors over the loutish, unfriendly men. Danny caught up with him.

"Those men didn't want to take our dinghy before," he said, "so I suppose it's safe enough to leave it now. We'll beach it and then tomorrow we'll spend all day with the horses."

They walked on silently until Danny said, "Weren't they horrid? We didn't do anything."

David kicked at a piece of dead coral, and Pauli rushed after it, but when it pricked her nose she left it alone.

"I'll bet they're criminals of some sort and frightened the police'll catch up with them," David remarked.

Danny was thrilled with this explanation of the men's rudeness.

"Pooh!" she said. "*I* don't care if the police *do* catch them. Come on, race you to the dinghy."

They dragged the dinghy well above any possible tide and set out for home.

"All I hope is that Percy's caught his own dinner and isn't waiting to complain to me about being neglected."

"If he is, don't you give in. Dad's right, he's a blackmailer."

"Whatever he is I love him," Danny answered happily. "I've got three special fish in the upper pool just for him —if he hasn't eaten them already!"

They reached the camp in time to join their parents for a swim, but they said nothing about their encounter with the strangers. The children felt that their parents might not want them to go to their island if they knew about the men on the nearby beach.

Mr. Delaney stood up as they reached the tent.

"So you're back—good. Now we'll all have a swim, although it's nearer to sunset than I like. But if we keep together we ought to be safe enough. How was your island?"

"Oh, fine," they said together in vague voices.

"How about taking the outboard and the big light and having a look at the coral tonight? That's when it's at its best. It'll be feeding and we might land on one of the outer reefs for a while. The tide's going to be low."

8

Where Are the Horses?

At certain angles the strong light David held could be turned so that the rays penetrated the water. His father drove the outboard, and Mrs. Delaney and Danny sat in the center, with Pauli prowling up and down, as they chugged toward the outer reefs.

Besides illuminating the sea creatures, the light showed where the dark masses of underwater reefs lay, and Mr. Delaney did his best to steer by David's yells and wavings. The sky clouded over, but there were still a few stars shining, their dazzle reflecting from the unlit waters, and the moon rose from behind scudding clouds.

It seemed to Danny that looking into the sea was like seeing the fishy life they knew in reverse. They often watched shoals of silvery sardines leaping from the water and making tiny fountains of drops from their myriad small bodies as some predator pursued them. Now just below the surface the light showed what seemed to be a regiment of sardines, maneuvering like mail-clad Lilliputian soldiers in perfect unison. They rose and sank, turned left or right, in perfect order.

Through the stillness came the steady booming of the sea on the great outer reef as they went toward the Coral Sea. Presently the light shone over the broad watery top of a reef, uncovered by the tide. It was very hot and the sea was calm.

"David, shine the light over to the right," Mrs. Delaney called.

David turned the light and they saw that the water at one spot looked flat and oily, moving in a faint, slow swirl. From the center of this a great ray broke the surface, the biggest they had seen, rising like some huge fleshy butterfly into the air until it seemed to blot out the sky. It came down to hit the water with a slapping boom that shivered and shook the outboard; then it disappeared beneath the surface. Pauli bounded onto Danny's lap, and Danny, awed by the creature's size, exclaimed, "Golly, I'm glad it didn't land on us!"

"We'll get out onto the reef for a while," said Mr. Delaney, letting the outboard slide gently up beside the reef. David handed the light to Danny while he fastened the rope.

"Be sure we're safely moored, son. We don't want to have to swim back from here!" Mr. Delaney called out to David.

David bent down and took another look at the rope. "It's fast. Come on, Dad, I'll hold her steady while you help Mother out."

The reef top, which could have been twenty or thirty feet across, looked rather like a dark, flooded garden. The whole surface was awash, and here and there lay what are called niggerheads: lumps of dead coral flung onto the reef by storms, ugly things bearing no relation to the flower beauty of the living coral. The reef gave out a strange chemical smell.

Mr. Delaney made them stand still and listen to the noises all about them. Danny carried Pauli because of the coral, and the whole family wore stout, pliant-soled sandals. As they stood listening they found that the reef creatures gave off a continuous medley of sounds, a crackling, barking, and grunting, that made David laugh.

"It's all *snap, crackle,* and *pop,*" he said, "like those advertisements for breakfast foods!"

"That snapping probably comes from pistol prawns, but I've no idea what the grunting is."

David flashed the light into the sea off the edge of the reef. Almost at once the bigger fish began to swarm.

"Keep the light on the reef," Mr. Delaney said. "If those big mullet swarm, all the night feeders will come after them, sharks and groupers, squid and barracuda."

Mrs. Delaney put in with, "Do you children realize

that we're treading on a vast living body made of untold millions of tiny creatures, all growing and feeding?"

The light shone on a sluglike sea hare creeping along the bottom of a pool, its shapeless body covered in a purple tracery as fine as lace. Then it lit up a cinnamon-colored anemone, its tentacles swaying, a giant living chrysanthemum looking for its prey.

At the far edge of the reef they stopped to admire the feeding corals. There were mushroom corals ten inches across, their undersides a mass of thin plates, and organ pipes, with their green polyps expanded to feed. Danny bent down and touched one, and the green flesh contracted, leaving a red, rigid skeleton. There was the blue of Heliopora; the intricate brain coral, green with red veins; the common yellow staghorn; and the cylindrical tubinaria. In the daytime the coral folded itself like sleeping flowers, but at night it bloomed fantastically as it fed from the gentle movement of the water. The family's eyes followed the light, and no one glanced at the sky above him until a roll of thunder and a fork of white lightning split across it.

"Come on, there's a storm on the way. Get back to the boat as quickly as you can."

Mr. Delaney took his wife's arm, and David held the light high to make a pathway ahead of them. Danny clutched Pauli, who was rather cross at not being put down on this fantastic playground.

A far-off moaning came to their ears as they scrambled into the boat. Without being told, everyone knew that a great storm wind moved in the darkness, growling over the face of the reef like some gigantic animal. The continuous noise of the reef died to a few faint sounds. Mr. Delaney started the engine as David slipped the rope.

"I hope we'll beat the storm home, but I doubt it. If it hits us, you two hold on to Pauli and get down in the bottom of the boat. Leave everything to David and me. Reef storms are fierce but soon over. With any luck we'll only be on the fringe of it."

The first squall struck in a few minutes. Danny, with her mother and Pauli, crouched down. The outboard made the fastest time possible and David put the light in its socket so as to have both hands free. Darkness pressed in like a solid thing and the light that had once seemed so bright was driven back by the denseness of the night.

Beneath the little boat the swell increased and Mr. Delaney tried to hold her side-on to the rising waves. Danny clung to Pauli with one hand, her mother with the other. She was uncomfortable but not afraid. The scream of the wind drew nearer, waves rose, and spray drenched them, and David baled away the shipped water. The storm was behind them and drove them in the direction of their own beach. When the worst of it struck, the little boat spun around, bucking and twisting like a wild horse. Then the approaching rain, roaring like an express train, raced down on them.

The storm was there and it broke in torrential rain, which made it impossible to be certain of their direction. They felt the prow touch sand. David leaped out into a downpour so heavy they all gasped for breath and saw each other only as gray shadows. They dragged the boat far up the beach and guessed at the direction of the tents. Holding hands, they struggled on, almost bumping into the big tent before they saw it. Inside the worst of the wind was baulked by the stout canvas walls straining inward, but the rain drummed down noisily. Trenches around the tent channeled off the water, and the returning family stood by the flap and dripped for a few minutes.

Danny looked up from squeezing out her hair. She smiled as she saw Pauli, who was not amused, shaking herself and lifting one disgusted paw after the other from the little puddles.

As quickly as the storm began, it stopped. All around them they heard the sound of running water, the patter of big drops as the dying wind swayed the trees, and strange sucking sounds as the thirsty earth drank up the rain, which had fallen too quickly to be absorbed immediately.

Wrapped in dry clothes and towels, the Delaney family soon felt better. David went to the tent flap. A watery moon was shining on the glistening land, and the clouds raced out of the sky as quickly as they had raced across it.

"Now we'll have a hot drink and then walk over to see if your tents have been as waterproof as ours."

"Poor Percy, I suppose he's a soppy mess somewhere. I do hope he's all right."

"Don't give him a thought—he'll see that he's all right!"

Now that it was over they all realized that they had rather enjoyed the adventure. Together they tramped across the spongy, trickling earth to Danny's tent. David led. He stooped to enter the tent flap, lit the lamp, and then turned, with a big grin on his face, to where the others stood.

"Don't worry about Percy, Danny. He's all right!"

Danny came forward. "Where? I can't see him—oh, goodness! What a clever boy!"

There, on her bed and all mixed up with the mosquito nets, squatted Percy, his bill turned back on his wing, sleeping peacefully.

"Well," Mrs. Delaney said firmly, "you can't share your bed with a pelican, Danny. I forbid it. So come back with us and sleep on the daybed tonight and let Percy sleep it off. Your bedclothes have to be washed tomorrow anyhow."

Danny looked gratefully at her mother. "Thanks, Mother. I'd so hate to move him, poor old boy."

Pauli suddenly discovered that Percy was sleeping on Danny's bed, which she considered her own. She rose up on her fat little hams and pressed her nose into the net and gave an indignant bark. Percy's eyelids trembled; he roused his feathers slightly and returned to dreamland.

Danny picked up Pauli, and after the family had established that David's bed and tent were intact, the others went back to the big tent, where Pauli, exhausted by all the excitement, snuggled against Danny and slept soundly.

In the morning Mr. Delaney had a temperature and his wife insisted that he must stay in bed. No one else was the worse for wear, but the children felt that they

should stay around the camp that day to be with their mother. However, they could not help worrying about the horses. Both David and Danny were tired after the stormy night—it was only at such times that they remembered they might still be suffering from the accident. They swam and lazed in between helping their mother and playing chess with their father.

The next day they were still needed, so they only

walked as far as one of the open spaces from which they had cut the first grass for the horses. It was muddy, but through the dark green of the old grass they could see vigorous blades of pale new grass. They knew that in a few days they would be able to cut enough to take a sackful to the horses.

"I'm afraid they'll be terribly wild again," said Danny.

"Don't forget that the storm will have made plenty of new growth on the island, too. They're probably getting fat and contented. They won't need us until they've eaten their own grass down again."

Once Mr. Delaney was up and about again he decided he must do rather less for a while. When he felt better he knew he was apt to forget he was still an invalid. He decided this was silly and that he must remember that he, as well as the rest of his family, was on the Reef to convalesce as well as to have a holiday. They lived largely on fish, shrimps, and oysters, supplemented by their large store of tinned vegetables, rice, and an occasional edible bird. Life was easy and comfortable, and the days went by almost too swiftly.

Several days after the storm the children were free to return to their island. They filled in the time by secretly making halters for the horses, swiping some of the long rawhide ropes from their stores.

"I suppose you kids want to see what the storm has done to your island," Mr. Delaney said one morning. "Would you like to leave Pauli with me? She's such company when I'm fishing."

When the children left, Mr. Delaney sat with Pauli on

his knees. He looked at his wife and said, "You know, Madge, I'm rather curious to know just what it is about that island that makes it so special."

"Yes, I've noticed the looks the children give each other when the island's mentioned."

Walking up the beach toward the dinghy, David said, "Dad's pretty cute and so's Mother. What a wonder they haven't suspected there's something on our island."

Apart from being rather messy, the dinghy had weathered the storm. They inspected it and then pushed their way through the jungle to cut grass. The rain and the hot sun had started up the growth, and the old gap was closely laced by tangled creepers and branches. The grass was long and green. It was tender and easy to cut and they soon filled the sack. They were both very excited at the thought of returning to the island.

"I wonder if the horses were afraid of the storm."

"They must have seen plenty of storms if they've been on the island for a year or two."

They waded ashore and tipped out the grass, calling, "Kip, kip!" but nothing happened. There was no whinnying; there were no anger noises from Old Bill, no leaves rustling on the hillside.

"They must be *somewhere*—why don't they come?" said Danny.

"How would I know?" David said rather crossly, because he was worried. "Come on, call louder—kip! *kip! KIP!*"

It was no use. "Surely the storm couldn't have driven them off the island, could it, David?"

"I don't think so. But it's odd—they always come so quickly when they hear us call. Perhaps they've had so much to eat here they're not interested in our grass any more."

"I'm sure they'd come if they could, and they must have heard us by now. What can we do?"

They thought for a while, then Danny said, "I know what I'm going to do. We can't go and leave them without searching the island—we must find out what's happened. I think we should go up their hill and look for them."

"You're right, but let's put the grass back in the sack. Otherwise it'll blow away and we ought to have something to give them when we do find them."

"If we find them," Danny said sadly, and her heart felt heavy with foreboding.

9

Old Bill to the Rescue

Having announced that they were going up the hill to look for the three horses, David called to Danny to wait.

"Hang on a sec. I'll get the rope and the halters out of the dinghy. We might need them."

"Oh, all right, but hurry."

Danny was suddenly filled with a premonition of evil. She waited impatiently while David took the halters they had made so secretly and the slender but infinitely strong rawhide rope out of the dinghy. He joined her, the ropes coiled on his shoulder, and they set off, pushing their way through the fresh, tangled greenness out of which they had so often seen the horses coming to them.

As they went scrambling through the thickets, torn by thorns and stumbling over fallen branches, they called, "Kip! Kip!" every now and again. There was no answer except the screams of seabirds from the rocks below. A covey of red-crowned fruit pigeons flew from a thicket and flitted about them, as did a flock of gray-breasted silvereyes. If they had not been so worried they would have delighted in the vivid fruit of the scurvy grass and the bamboolike supplejack with its fawn blooms.

They reached the peak of the miniature mountain, and in every small space the grass was new and green, thrusting toward the light, and none of it had been eaten down. The children stopped to get their breath back, the steamy heat rising about them. They had made fast time through the clawed green things, but now they had to decide where to descend.

"Oh, David, I'm so nervous for them!"

"Come on, let's go straight down. Listen!"

They held their breath. Somewhere a horse snorted. The sound was not repeated, so they started down the steep slope, digging their heels into the soft earth and getting tangled in creepers. Halfway down they heard a muffled thudding, but they hurried on. Perspiration stung their eyes; their hands were torn, their legs scratched and plastered in mud. The side of the hill was spongy with rain, so it was hard to hurry.

Danny led, squeezing her eyes together against the stinging saltiness, when her foot went down into nothing. She gave a yell and threw herself backward. David, who was just behind her, grabbed her shoulder, dug in his heels, and hung on. Danny sat on the ground, her feet under her, and looked up at David.

"I was nearly over the edge of something. Can we pull the bushes away and look—oh, be careful, David!"

On hands and knees they began to tug at the bushes. Falling away from them, and as steep as a cliff, they saw what looked like a greasy slide of black mud, which had been hidden from them by bushes growing right up to the brink.

They crawled cautiously forward and looked over the edge. There had been a landslide. It was almost as if a black mouth had opened up and swallowed the greenery except for the fringe along the top. The children looked down at the vertical slope.

"David, look!" Danny gasped. "Down there, something's moving—it can't be—yes, it is. It *is* one of the horses!"

David peered downward. "There're two horses! The poor brutes—look, they're in a kind of crevice of slippery mud. We must do something. Come on, let's get down level with the other side—it's lower there."

They began to edge around the dreadful slope, treading warily, afraid of starting another landside of the water-soaked earth.

"Poor things," Danny gasped between her efforts to follow David. "They must be starving. They must have been there for days. And I wonder where the third horse is—and which one it'll be."

They reached the level where the crevice began and worked around it to the lower side. It looked as if there must have been a hollow under the earth to make the cave-in that formed such a terrible trap. The landslide had been stopped by a solid platform of earth, and along this platform the bushes were trampled down and the ground flattened.

At the far end, head flung high and eyes distraught, stood Old Bill. Obviously he had tried to find a way down to his two precious young ones, but fortunately for him he had been unable to do so. Bill's ribs stuck out and his eyes stared. His distress overrode his dislike and fear of humans. The children were very touched that, with all the fresh young grass about, the old horse had been too distressed to eat.

"David, how can we help them?"

"We must think of something. The crevice isn't very deep from this side," David said. "I'll go around it and try to find a place where we could throw down bushes for their hooves to grip on."

Danny walked quietly toward Old Bill, her heart so shaken by his misery that she did not stop to think that he might have reverted to his old dangerous self. He stood perfectly still; then as she neared him his ears flattened and his head dropped; he snaked his neck in the terrifying way of a killer horse. But Danny, her heart full of compassion for him, did not stop. Very gently she approached that swinging head, and all the power she had over animals, the power whose roots sprang from her real love of them, seemed to fold about her like a shield.

The horse's gaunt, ugly head ceased to sway and the ears came forward. Danny stood beside him, her arms around his thin neck, her face against his scarred hide, as she whispered comforting words of love and sympathy to him. Her fingers circled those wicked old ears, while her small freckled face, full of loving concern, pressed against the bony nose of the head whose bared teeth had so often menaced her.

"Poor old boy. We'll get the young ones out, don't you

worry. David'll find some way." Old Bill sighed and snuffed and was comforted. "Now," Danny went on, "I must go and help David and you mustn't get in our way."

"Danny!" David shouted. "Come over here."

He was at the far end of the crevice and Danny hurried to him. Old Bill shambled after her like any cart horse. David looked up from where he crouched on his knees.

"Look, it's not really very high here," he said. "The trouble is it's as slippery as glass. You can see how they've been struggling to get out, pawing the sides and slipping back. But if we could lower it a bit, then give them something for their hooves to grip on, they might make it." His voice was doubtful.

"What's that big mud-covered bump in the way?"

"That's the trouble with this end. It's a rock. If we could only move that, then a lot of this mess would fall away and they'd get out easily enough."

"Why can't we move it?"

"Because it's much too heavy," David said patiently.

"Perhaps it's too heavy for us, but it mightn't be too heavy for Bill to pull it away."

"Old Bill! How could we make him pull?"

"We could use the rope and halters, and I think I could make him pull."

"It's worth a try. It's been five days since the storm and they must be getting weaker all the time and need water as much as they need food."

"Give me a halter and I'll put it on Bill. D'you think you can fix a rope around his neck and onto the rock?"

"Yes, the rock's pretty rough once you scrape the mud away. Give me five minutes and then bring Bill—no, wait, help me put down bushes so that his hooves can grip."

Together they tore and chopped bushes until they made a solid path along which they hoped Bill would go.

"I hope the rock won't bound out and hit him on the hocks," Danny said nervously.

"I hope not. I think he'll only have to give the rock a good jerk. You can see it's the keystone for the whole lot. The bank'll crumble once it's moved and then the horses should be able to get out."

Danny stood back and looked at the bush-covered ground. "There, that ought to be all right. Now I'll put the halter on him while you fix the traces."

Bill let Danny come up to him; then he backed and snorted at the halter. But she talked and cajoled him until she could slip it over his ears. He stood tossing his head up and down, and Danny put gentle pressure on the halter until, looking rather surprised at himself, he began to trot after her. She found David with the strange traces ready, and together they worked patiently, until finally the old horse allowed himself to be harnessed.

"That rope around his shoulders'll cut into him," Danny said, and the children tugged off their shirts and wrapped them around the rope at the points where Bill's shoulders must take the pull. But when they wanted him to begin pulling it was another matter. He backed and jumped and sprang forward until the traces tightened, and then he reared backward, but he would not give a steady pull.

"Oh, dear, what can we do? He won't pull!"

"He'll break the ropes if he doesn't stop that. Come on, let's try again."

The pathway of twigs and leaves was beaten sodden and flat. Whenever David neared Bill's head he played up, so he left Danny to cling to the halter, while she begged the old horse to pull.

Down in the slimy pit the two young horses, worn out from repeated efforts to struggle up the slippery bank, stood with drooping heads. Their bodies were plastered with black mud, their hooves heavy with it, their spirits at the lowest ebb.

"All right now, Bill, come on, help your friends." But Bill decided he'd had enough. He shook his head, rose up and pawed the air, then gave a bound forward. Out came the rock with a terrific *ssluurp* of mud. The rope slipped off it, and as Danny was jerked forward too, still clinging to the halter, David realized that they had won!

Slowly the messy earth caved in. The young horses, after huddling together at the far end, found themselves able to clamber out of the horrible black mouth that had been their prison, and might have become their grave.

"We've done it!" David yelled, and Bill stopped and swung Danny around after him as he saw his two weary, filthy friends emerging from the crevice. He broke into a gallop and Danny ran after him until the halter was torn from her hands. She stopped beside David, panting.

"Oh, dear, I'll catch him in a minute," she said. "The old boy really did it even if it was an accident!"

David looked at his exhausted, mud-spattered sister. She was nearly as much of a mess as were the horses.

"You were great, Danny. All the time he was playing up he still took good care not to hurt you. Didn't you notice that?"

Danny looked amazed. "I never thought for a minute he'd hurt me. He just wouldn't obey me."

"Well, the horses are all right now."

"I must get the halter off Bill—he might trip over it."

"Not him, the old monkey. Let's go and see what they're doing and then we'll have a swim. Gosh, you do look filthy!"

"So do you—oh, I'm frightful!" Danny peered down at herself.

They followed the horses down the hill and found all three below on the edge of a strip of sand on which they had been rolling. Cloud's delicate silvery-gray, dappled hide still looked dirty. Old Bill was proudly in control, trailing the halter, and Manta cropped eagerly at the strip of grass between the hillside and the beach.

Bill stood as docilely as an old stock horse as Danny went to him to remove the halter. She stroked and petted him and told him how clever he was, and he, like any civilized horse, turned his rakish old head and nibbled at her with soft lips. Danny laughed as his nibbling tickled her and she remembered the great yellow fangs with which he used to menace her. The youngsters were too busy with the grass to do more than flinch away when David put his hand on their sides, and giving a kind of sideways curtsy, they began to feed again.

"I think that black trap's done more to tame them than we could have done in another month."

As it was the first time that Danny and David had been at that end of the island, they looked curiously about them. They walked to where they were almost at the other end before they decided to go into the sea off a little sandy beach opposite where the dinghy was anchored.

The children moved lazily in the water and gradually the mud dissolved from them.

"Let's see what the bottom's like here," David called, and they turned like young porpoises and jackknifed down. They came up, puffing and blowing.

"What a funny reef that is down there," Danny began.

"That's not a reef, dope, that's a wreck. It's so old it's crusted with coral. We'll need our masks and flippers, though. You just watch out tomorrow! I'll bet there's treasure in there somewhere!"

10

Treasure!

The sea, full of debris, caused a nasty coral cut on David's foot, so it was actually a month before the children were able to look for treasure in the wreck off their island. But the weeks between were not wasted, and they spent them taming the horses.

One sunny morning Danny and David stood in front of their parents, saying, "We're inviting you to call at Wild Horse Island this afternoon!"

Mr. Delaney smiled up at his children. "About time too! We thought you were never going to invite us and we didn't want to invite ourselves. Wild horses, eh?"

Danny beamed at him. "We were clever to pick you and Mother for our parents!"

Each day since the rescue of the young horses the children had handled them. Even Bill was becoming as tame as a pet pony. They fastened grass sacks across the youngsters' backs, then finally mounted them without saddles or bridles. Steering by knees and voices, they rode them around the island. Old Bill allowed Danny to ride him, but he shied away from David.

The elder Delaneys were invited to come over in the midafternoon. The children wanted to give the horses a good brush down. Both Danny's and David's hairbrushes had disappeared from their tents—they made a good substitute for horse brushes!

Pauli was friendly with all the horses, and in the way of many horses and dogs, she and Cloud had a special friendship. Showers and storms kept the island grass green, and the children did not have to take extra food over from the mainland.

Now they hurried off to the dinghy. David's foot was completely healed, and when they had finished with the horses they wanted to have another look at the wreck to see if it was worth showing to their father. They collected their underwater gear and ran along the long sandy beach, with Pauli galloping ahead.

They rowed out to the island, and by the time they'd given the horses an extra rubdown the sun was striking down through the water in shafts of afternoon light.

"Come on, let's explore the wreck," David said.

The wreck, now only ribs and planks held together by coral growths, looked like one of those flower floats used in processions. It was only about fifteen feet down, but real work was required to explore it thoroughly when they had to come up for air every two or three minutes. Above their heads the surface looked like a sheet of silver paper, and the sea was very warm as they swam among the shoals of fish.

They carried a metal-tipped coral pick for prizing away any bulge that looked interesting and began the hard work of trying to free something that appeared to be a small, metal-bound chest. Every movement was hampered by the drag and weight of the water around them. When they could not free or move it they abandoned the chest and tried to knock the coral off a smaller, but equally interesting-looking bump.

With a fierce grunt David finally succeeded in tearing the coral lump free. He shot up to the surface, with his lungs fairly bursting. Danny followed him up and they swam ashore, put the object on the sand, and went to work with the coral pick, being careful not to injure whatever had caused the formation.

When at last a piece of coral crumbled away they saw the shine of gold and were so excited they went back to work with great vigor. Finally, with pieces of coral still attached, with some parts almost black and other patches unmistakably yellow, David held in his hand a beautiful, heavily engraved goblet. It was a wine cup, which they thought might be centuries old.

"Come on," David yelled, "let's meet Mother and Dad."

As they scrambled into the dinghy they saw the outboard coming from the opposite beach, and Danny rowed furiously, while David stood up in the rocking dinghy, brandishing the goblet and yelling, "Look! Mother! Dad! We've found treasure!"

"Where did you find it?" Mr. Delaney yelled back across the water.

David, still brandishing the goblet shouted, "From a wreck on the other side of the island. It's real gold"—

another flourish of the goblet—"and there's a chest we can't move. I'll bet it's full of treasure!"

When the boats bumped, Mr. Delaney took the goblet and examined it, with Mrs. Delaney peering over his shoulder. They were both as excited as the children.

"Let's go straight back to camp where we can deal with it properly," said Mr. Delaney.

"But what about the horses—the island?"

"We'll see the whole thing tomorrow. Come on, leave the dinghy opposite and come back with us." Mr. Delaney turned his head and pointed to a thin line of smoke that seemed to trickle upward from among the trees at the far end of the beach. "Looks as if there are Abos here."

David shook his head. "No, it's a couple of beach-combers. They were so grumpy and unfriendly when we spoke to them that we didn't mention them to you."

"They called Pauli a mongrel!" complained Danny.

"Oh, well," said her father, laughing, "there's plenty of room for us all—no need for us to bother each other."

The children pulled the dinghy high up on the beach and rushed back to jump into the outboard. Once back in camp, half an hour's hard work showed them what a beautiful object they had found.

"It's the real thing," Mr. Delaney told them. "I think we'd better leave it now and let a jeweler do the rest when we get back to Brisbane."

That night, fired by their successful treasure hunting, the children decided to get up early and return to the island and try again to raise the treasure chest. If they found it full of precious stones, what a surprise it would be to greet their parents with!

They were away so early and so quietly that even Pauli didn't see them go, and in their excitement they forgot her. Rushing along the beach, they remembered that the dinghy would not be in its usual place, as they had left it past the next headland, on the beachcombers' beach. It was only a little after sunrise when they scrambled around the rocky headland. The beach was empty, the dinghy gone, and they instantly thought of the churlish men. But why would they take the dinghy?

"David," Danny said, "they must've been watching and heard you shouting that we'd found treasure."

"Yes, that must be it. Look over at the island."

Danny followed David's gaze. On the little island beach their dinghy lay on the sand.

"The horses—" Danny began anxiously.

"I don't suppose they'll bother about the horses. I'll bet they're looking for the treasure chest. I wonder if they swim well."

"I suppose they thought we'd be along at our usual time. That would have given them a chance to get the chest and put the dinghy back as if they'd never touched it."

David looked at her seriously and said, "I wish you'd go home, Danny. I'm not going to let those two get away with this so easily. I'm going to wait for them."

"Then so am I." Danny sat down determinedly on the rocks. "But what can we do, David?"

"I don't know. I'll think of something. We could easily

swim across the channel, except for the sharks. I guess that'd be a silly thing to do."

"Mother and Dad'd be very angry if we did."

"We can only wait. I don't see the horses."

"Look!" Danny stood up excitedly. "There are the men and—oh, David, they're carrying *our* chest!"

They watched angrily as the two men, with the small, heavy chest between them, came over the rise toward the dinghy. The bushes on the slope of the hill began to lash about violently. One of the men yelled something and the bushes parted. Barnacle Bill, his killer fury upon him, came charging down the slope, giving his terrible, neighing scream.

The men promptly dropped the chest where the water met the beach, and the lid jerked open. They did not even notice it but hurled themselves toward the dinghy. They scrambled into it, making it rock wildly. David sprang to his feet.

"Old Bill to the rescue again!" he exclaimed. "Look! Those men don't know much about boats—they nearly capsized her."

Old Bill plunged into the sea, stretched out his neck, and bared his teeth as the dinghy bucked away. One of the men seized an oar and raised it as though to smash it down on the horse's skull. Danny screamed, "Oh, don't!" Bill ducked and gripped the edge of the dinghy with his teeth and shook it. The man overbalanced and the oar came down harmlessly. Bill let go and turned and swam for the shore, while the dinghy turned neatly over and deposited both men into the sea, shouting and grabbing

at the slippery keel. Bill trotted up and down the little beach, daring them to swim ashore!

"Look at those idiots!" David shouted excitedly. "They don't know how to right the dinghy and Bill won't let them land.

All that splashing and noise'll bring every shark in the channel!"

"Oh, David, they're horrible men, but we can't leave them to the sharks. Tell them how to turn the dinghy."

David cupped his hands and yelled instructions, but the two men were too panicky to listen. David's sunburned face was very serious as he turned to his sister.

"Danny, please stay here," he said. "They'll drown or
—or bring the sharks. I'd rather go now before that
happens."

"Oh, David!"

Danny watched her brother dive into the water. Then,
her face very white and determined, she went in after
him, swimming as fast and as silently as she could. Once
she paused, and her frightened eyes saw a triangular
black fin, made small by distance, and then another
. . . coming closer. . . . She turned her head and
swam on.

Neither of the children remembered much about that

swim or the rescue. They realized that the men were in-
sane with their fear of sharks. David had to slap and
shout at them to get them off the dinghy to right it. Then
he found Danny beside him.

With the dinghy righted, the men lacked the strength
to get into it and David was afraid they would turn it
over again. He got the dark man in, but the fair-haired
man sobbed and shouted and kept slipping back into the
sea. The other man made no attempt to help. Then,
through the churning water, the children saw a misty
gray shape. It seemed to glide past the crying man and
he gave a piercing yell. They saw a trickle of blood seep-
ing into the water from his back, where the sharp teeth
of the shark had nicked an inch-sized piece of flesh in an
experimental way.

The shock acted like an uncoiling spring in the terrified man. He sprawled over the side and fell onto the
boards. David thrust Danny down to the bottom of the
boat and grabbed an oar he had saved. He saw the blunt,
evil head and tiny pig eyes as the shark leaped almost out of the water after the man. Below the rocking
dinghy the sea seethed and boiled with dark, supple
shapes.

"Is he much hurt?" Danny stared fearfully at the
sharks, which were drawn by the blood and were moving
in the water, like smooth, dark metal.

"He's only frightened," David said briefly. "Come on,
or they'll have us all in the sea, and this time no one will
get out."

They got the overladen dinghy to the mainland beach

and pushed the men out. "Shock, I suppose," David said. "They're as silly as rabbits."

The dark man muttered a confused thanks, and they both staggered up the beach. David put his arm around his sister. "Come on, Danny, we'll go on home. You know I couldn't have righted the dinghy on my own. It was you who saved us all."

Danny shook her head. "I was terrified."

"Well, you did it. What about the treasure chest?"

"Let's leave it. We have the dinghy. Anyway, I don't suppose the men would go back."

After giving to their parents a mild version of what had happened and having some sharp looks directed at their pale faces, they went to bed early and set off next morning to get the horses ready for their parents' visit.

They found the chest wedged against a rock, the lid open, and the insides half full of a weedy mess. "Here, give me the pick. I wonder what's in there besides our treasure."

David moved the pick around. "Hey, Danny! There's something alive in here—help me tip out this mess, but look out for diamonds!"

What they found after they had gingerly washed away all the mess was not diamonds, but the hideous form of a deadly stonefish. With a toadlike face and weed twisted among the venomous spines along its back, it had a horrid grayish web all over its squat body. It lay there, a dreadful poisonous creature, and the children knew that one touch of its cruel spines could bring death in twenty minutes with heart-stopping pain.

"A fine treasure!" Danny said indignantly. "Do shut the lid. Dad'll want to see it, I suppose, but we mustn't let Pauli near it."

"We'll never know what was really in the chest," David said sadly. "The tide could have washed it out when it washed that awful thing in!"

"Come on, David, let's find the horses. I only hope nothing else awful happens today."

11

Farewell to the Island

The children sat down on the rocks by the small beach and waited for the outboard to bring their parents and Pauli. They had groomed the horses. Now they looked disgustedly at the chest holding the hideous stonefish instead of jewels.

"There they are!" Danny called, pointing toward the headland. Coming around it, the outboard chugged along. They waved to their parents, then ran to the other side of the island and mounted Cloud and Manta. Old Bill seemed to have forgotten his hatred of mankind, but even so, the children were a little worried about his reception of their parents.

When they rode over the rise toward the beach, Bill trotted behind. The Delaneys saw their son and daughter, saddleless and bridleless, each astride a beautiful young horse, while a third horse, a villainous-looking, four-legged Long John Silver, followed them.

Mr. Delaney stopped the engine, and the outboard drifted up onto the beach. He helped his wife out. This was the moment when Danny had feared Old Bill might forget his manners. She slipped off Cloud and put her arms reassuringly around Bill's neck. The man-eating gleam came into his eyes, and his ears went back. Danny gave a spring and landed on his back. Perhaps an audience meant something to Bill from his early days. The old horse pulled himself together and moved quietly and proudly as if he were in a show-ring.

"Aren't they lovely?" Danny asked. "You can pat Cloud, but be careful of Bill—he doesn't like strangers."

"What an understatement!" David thought, his anxious eye on the horse. But Mr. Delaney had his own magic with horses. He had not been among them all his life for nothing. First he patted Manta, then Cloud; then he came over to Bill, and Danny's heart beat faster.

Bill stood proudly, and only his eyes showed a flicker of concern, his stance obviously that of an old show-ring performer. Mr. Delaney went to his head, stroked him, and spoke quietly, as a judge might speak to a nervous horse, running his firm hands over the scarred old hide.

"Come over here, Madge," he called to his wife.

Mrs. Delaney left Manta and came over to be introduced to Bill. He stood quietly and she exclaimed at his scars.

"What do you think made those scars, Daddy?" Danny asked.

"Some brutal rider made those on his ribs, but if it is possible for him to have escaped them, I'd think those scars, the long ones, might come from sharks. I don't suppose you know how they got on the island, do you?"

"We thought they might have been shipwrecked."

"That's possible. Many horse-carrying ships have foundered on the reefs. I'd say Bill got those long scars fighting sharks off himself and the youngsters while swimming to the island."

Mrs. Delaney broke in. "Wasn't the poor old fellow very wild when you found him, Danny?"

"Oh, yes, he was, Mother. That's why it was so long before we could ask you and Dad to our island."

"What are you going to do about them when we all leave?" Mr. Delaney asked.

"Oh, Daddy, I'm sure Captain Morris would ship them."

"But you have your own horses at home. Anyway, your Old Bill wouldn't be much use to anyone."

Danny gave a wail of protest. "Oh, you couldn't separate them," she said. "Bill would die of loneliness. He adores the other two. Please, please, don't leave him behind."

"Well, we'll have to see. Now, let's take a look at the island."

But the day was spoiled for Danny. It had never entered her head that the old horse might be left behind, deserted by everyone, to die of loneliness. She followed the others, romping and scrambling to the top of the hill. Danny kept thinking of the quiet way her father had spoken. She knew he had really meant it.

Mr. Delaney looked back and asked David, "Where's Danny?"

"I guess she's with the horses."

"I hope she's not sulking because I won't take Bill

back with us. What could we do with an old bag of bones like that?"

"Danny loves him because he *is* an old bag of bones," Mrs. Delaney said quietly.

"Oh, Madge, be sensible. He'd be safe here with the island all to himself."

"He might be safe," said David, "but he wouldn't be happy without the others."

Mr. Delaney looked down at his son. "Not you too, David. I thought you'd have some sense. You go on—I'm going to wait here to speak to Danny."

"Dick, don't be hard on Danny—be gentle with her."

"When have I ever been hard on Danny? But someone must show some common sense."

David and his mother walked on and Mr. Delaney sat down on a tangle-topped log and waited. Danny, her feet dragging and her heart heavy, came up the hill. Old Bill walked behind her. Every now and again he bumped the back of her neck, nibbling at her, so that she turned and stroked him, kissing his old scarred nose while the tears poured down her face. She didn't see her father until she was almost on top of him.

"Wait a minute, Danny, I want to talk to you," he said.

She looked at him with sullen, red-rimmed eyes. At that moment he did not seem to be the father she knew. She felt very forlorn. She did not speak but sat stiffly on the log a little way from him. Pauli, panting furiously, climbed up the log and, walking along it, jumped into

Danny's lap. Danny gathered the little dog into her arms
and waited.

"Danny," her father began in that quiet voice she
dreaded, and which made her look back at him defiantly
because she felt helpless and alone. Why weren't David

and her mother helping to save Bill after all the horrible
things that men had done to him in the past?

Her father's voice went on, "You know I'm not going
to ship your old horse along with the other two. You're
being very foolish. Perhaps you'd rather we left all three
horses here."

Suddenly Danny realized how much she loved the
beautiful Cloud and how David cared about Manta. But

above everything else she thought of the bewildered loneliness of Old Bill, who already had so much to forgive
man for. Now he would have to add something more:
the breaking of his old heart.

"Yes, I would rather they all stayed here together,"
she said in a tired little voice.

"Now, Danny, don't be silly. I'm willing to ship those
two splendid young horses, but the old one must stay.
There'll be plenty of grass for one horse and he'll be safe
on the island. I'm sorry, but that is my final decision. I
don't want to hear any more about it."

Mr. Delaney rose and walked after the others. Danny's tear-dimmed eyes watched his retreating back. De-
spair filled her heart. Pauli yawned and licked her chin,
then yawned again and jumped off her lap and began
sniffing about in the grass. Danny's eyes were blank. She
was shut in in an unhappy world of her own. Then she
heard Pauli's sharp yaps coming from the grass about
ten yards in front of her.

Danny's eyes focused on Pauli's plump little back
view. Her tail was wagging like a flag in her excitement
and she made little forward bounces as she yapped. A
copper-colored head with cold eyes and a flickering
tongue rose in the air above Pauli. Danny knew the head
belonged to that six feet of sinuous death that bushmen
call a tiger snake. Her sorrow-dulled mind became alert,
as in a flash she remembered that the tiger snake is one
of the most venomous snakes in the world, and one of
the very few that will follow and attack a retreating foe.

Danny did not even hear her own shout of "Pauli!

Pauli, come here!" but something in her voice made that intrepid hunter turn and rush to her. She bent and swept Pauli up, her eyes on the snake. With its strong muscles surged together and its wicked head dropped, the swirling body of the snake propelled itself forward in a muscular movement of grace and power. It was coming in to attack.

Like all snakes it was deaf and did not hear her shout, but another animal heard it. Danny sprang to her feet, clutching Pauli. Knowing it would be useless to run, she nevertheless turned and jumped onto the log. Then she heard a sound she had heard before: the screaming neigh of a charging horse.

For one awful instant she measured the onrushing, narrow copper head and estimated that it would strike midway up her shins. The next instant Barnacle Bill burst like a fury out of the bushes. He, too, had heard the fear in Danny's voice and he didn't hesitate. With pounding hooves and tossing mane he bore down on the muscular whiplash of copper that lifted a third of its long body and turned to meet him, the death-filled head swaying, poised for its lightning strike.

Danny's shout had been heard by more than the dog and the horse. It reached her parents' and David's ears. Without a word they all turned. Tearing their way through bushes and trailing vines, they rushed toward the sound. Reaching the edge of the clearing, they saw Old Bill, his own head as fierce and flat as the head of some giant serpent, rushing in for the kill. He bared his yellow teeth, thrust his head forward, and caught the

copper body a few inches behind the head. Holding and shaking the snake, he reared and tore at the dangling body with his hooves, shaking and beating it until, with an upward fling of his head, he loosed his hold. The broken, pounded body of his enemy fell limply to the ground a dozen feet away.

Now poor Danny was truly frantic. Bill had saved her

life. Was it to cost him his own? Had the fang-filled head managed to inflict as much as a scratch during the snorting and shaking and pounding? If so, Barnacle Bill was doomed.

"Daddy—David—*do* something!" she wailed, flinging her arms about the shaggy neck. Her father and brother ran their hands carefully over the horse's neck and head, his chest and legs. Mr. Delaney stood back.

"I don't know, Danny," he said. "It's impossible to find the fang marks, but if he's been bitten, there should be a damp patch of venom on his hide. Try not to be upset—we can only wait. In ten minutes we'll know."

The family sat along the log, with Pauli in Mrs. Delaney's lap, while Danny stood, her body trembling with fear, her arms around the horse's scarred neck. Cloud and Manta came to the edge of the clearing and began cropping the grass. Bill enjoyed the fuss Danny made over him; he sighed and snuffed, and once he flung up his head as if he were listening, and Danny's heart missed a beat.

The minutes passed slowly. Mr. Delaney stared at his watch. Ten minutes . . . Old Bill was still on his feet . . . better give him another minute to be sure . . . eleven minutes . . . Bill dropped his head and began to munch the grass.

"That's it! He's all right, Danny! Danny, listen to me, he's—"

Danny turned around; she saw her father's face and she knew. She ran to him and he put his arms around her. "It's all right, Danny. Everything's all right," he said.

She lifted her tear-stained, freckled face. "You won't leave him behind now?"

Her father pushed the damp streaks of hair away from her forehead and shook his head. "I'll tell you what, darling. Bill's going to have the best accommodation the ship can offer. When we get home he's going to have the star stall always, and none of us is ever going to forget that he risked his life to save yours. But for him, our summer on Wild Horse Island might have ended in tragedy. Now, when the *Captain Cook* arrives, we'll be taking home only the happiest memories."

The deck of the *Captain Cook* vibrated gently. Below, the three horses were eating their supper. Barnacle Bill had submitted to having the wide canvas band put around his belly to swing him aboard, because Danny adjusted it and Danny was waiting to undo it when he was swung on deck.

Now she stood beside Captain Morris, gazing across the sunset-touched Reef waters. She looked brown and sturdy, unlike the thin, white-faced waif of six months before. She held Pauli on the deck rail in front of her, while high in the sky floated the tiny, silver-white bird she was sure was Percy.

"Glad to be going home, Danny?"

Danny thought for a moment. "Yes, but—" She gave a regretful sigh. "I'll never *ever* forget our summer on Wild Horse Island."